LYDIA ARLINGTON

AND THE AQUARIAN MYSTERY

DANIELLE RENEE WALLACE

Secrets are in store,

Danielle Renee Wallace

To Dad, Mom, Nick, and Ethan:

Thank you so much, Dad, for your help with everything. I appreciate your ideas and your memories of Wilsonville, as well as your advice and edits. Without your help, Wilsonville wouldn't be the same in this story.

Mom, I'm grateful for the help you've given me as I've written this book. Thank you for finding the time to read everything, give me suggestions, and catch those sometimes-crazy errors.

Nick, thank you for taking the time to be my editor. You didn't just read my book; you edited it. That's no small task, and your jokes made editing a lot more fun. I really appreciate it.

Ethan, while you didn't help me with this book, you have helped me by being a wonderful big brother. I'm grateful to have you as a sibling. Thank you for all that you've done.

TABLE OF CONTENTS

1	The Belonging of the Past	1
2	A Possibly Dangerous Idea	6
3	Away from the Stables	21
4	Another Clue	32
5	Stranger!	48
6	Snowflakes and Snickerdoodles	54
7	The Pursuit of Evidence	70
8	Paths of the Woods	82
9	Broken Glass	94
10	Springtime	120

THE BELONGING OF THE PAST
Chapter 1

"Come here, Charity!" I shouted to my friend and close comrade. That was my dog. Charity was a sweet little puppy that I had owned for the last three years. She has black, brown, and white spots. My parents bought her for me shortly before their passing. Since then, I've been living with my grandmother—my mother's mother—Lydia, whom I just so happen to be named after. After my parents' death, I had always wanted to know more about what they were like as children, but Grandmother wouldn't tell me much.

Anyway, I had just finished school about an hour or so before, and Charity and I were headed to our favorite place—our secret place. Charity barked happily and followed me as I ran down the sidewalk. Turning a corner, I headed into an alley, turned again, and walked to a secluded part of town nobody goes to that often. It can be a *little* scary, but I just *love* adventure—which, as my grandmother told me, isn't always a good thing. Not to mention, I'm rather curious. A big, yellow school bus came into view, and I smiled to myself, slowing my pace as my dog stayed close to my heels.

Cheerfully, I neared the school bus—which has been abandoned for years—and managed to push open the door. I had to be *very* careful because the bus was crammed full of books which would tumble out should I be careless. I never did know how they got there. Despite my best efforts, one of the books did indeed fall out, landing on my foot. That one was enough for a few others to tumble out, followed by some more.

"Oh!" I sputtered, trying to stop the avalanche from falling.

I successfully got the books to cease tumbling and pushed all of them back into the bus. Sitting down on the school bus steps, I relaxed for a moment.

"Phew! That's finished, isn't it, Charity?" I asked.

Charity let out a happy bark and hopped onto my lap.

"Good dog!" I told her—even if she was a little large for my lap.

Running my fingers through her soft fur, I breathed in her cute puppy scent that all dogs have. I hummed a tune softly as she snuggled up into my arms, dozing off. Letting Charity sleep, I tossed my brown braid over my shoulder, picked up one of my beloved books, and began reading.

A cold breeze blew by, and I secured my warm hat on my head more firmly. It was winter, so I'd expect to be slightly frozen by now. I loved it here anyway.

Because I had already brought some of my possessions to the school bus, it was like Charity and I had our own secret place to play. There was even a small chest my grandmother gave me for my birthday a couple of years ago.

Opening her big, brown eyes, Charity woke up from her rest and leaped off my lap, stretching.

"Did you sleep well?" I asked her, scratching behind her ears. She wagged her tail in response, and I smiled at her.

"Well, let's get going, girl. Grandmother must be waiting for us," I told my dog, rising to leave.

However, as I was about to go, Charity crawled under the bus and let out a small bark. Crouching down, I craned my neck, looking under the bus. I saw a book! Charity touched it with her nose. I must not have seen it when I picked up the others. Grabbing it, I quickly recognized it as the first book that had fallen out of the bus when I opened the door. I hadn't ever read it before, and it didn't have a title. The book is made of brown leather and has a golden buckle with a keyhole. Raising my eyebrow, I wondered whose this was and where its key could be. Being the curious girl I am, I remembered that I had a key in the chest my grandmother gave me.

Of course, it won't work, right?

I was determined to give it a chance, though. Digging through the horde of books, I pulled out the small chest. Opening it, I took out the silver key and sat down on the bus steps, Charity jumping up onto my lap.

I laughed softly and picked up the leather book. Sticking the key into the keyhole, I turned it. The book's buckle unlocked, and I gasped.

"It actually worked!" I exclaimed in amazement.

I excitedly opened the book to the first page and gasped—yet again—this time at the name written on it: *Liliana Adams*. That was my mother's name before she got married. I could hardly believe what I had just read! Quickly, I turned another page. The pages were covered in pretty writing—*handwriting*. It was a diary!

As I read the beginning sentences, I realized it *had* to be my mother's diary! Just reading through the first few pages, I learned all kinds of things about her. She wrote it when she was a girl—about twelve, which is how old I was—and she had a dog, like me. Her dog's name was Asher. Also, she loved to read. She reminded me of myself.

Could Mother and the bus be connected somehow?

Standing up from the bus steps, I smiled as I tucked the diary under my arm.

"I think I'll show my grandmother the diary," I said aloud. "Maybe she'll tell me more about my mother. Perhaps she might even know if the bus is linked to all this."

There was only one way to find out, and I knew just what that way was.

"Come on, Charity. Let's go home…"

I guess dreams really can come true.

A Possibly Dangerous Idea

Chapter 2

"Grandmother!" I panted breathlessly as I swung open the door to the house my grandma and I lived in.

Charity let out a happy bark as she came in with me, and I unbuckled her collar. Grandmother, Charity, and I live in a small town called Wilsonville, which is in Nebraska. I always found it cozy and safe here.

I pulled off my navy-blue winter hat, and I slipped off my light-brown ankle boots.

"Grandmother!" I shouted again, hanging up my denim jacket. I dropped my light-brown, leather backpack (which had blue and white stripes on the flaps, as well as lace) off by the door. Skipping, I made my way out of the hallway.

"I'm in the kitchen, Lydia!" Grandmother cheerfully replied.

I nodded—although Grandmother couldn't see me nod because I was walking through the living room.

Our house was snug but welcoming. It had two bedrooms, a kitchen, a living room, a small laundry room, and a bathroom—oh, and the pantry, too! The fireplace was crackling merrily in the living room as I headed to the kitchen.

I breathed in the scent of bread baking, mixed with the aroma of sugar cookies in the oven. My grandma loves to cook, and I love to help her. I guess you could say we make a pretty good team!

"Grandmother, you'll never guess what I've found!" I chirped happily as I hopped into the kitchen, Charity lying down close to Grandmother. The reason why Charity was lying at Grandmother's feet was that Grandmother was cutting potatoes. Knowing my dog, Charity likely wanted a treat. My grandma teases Charity for being a beggar.

"What did you find?" Grandmother asked me, a smile tugging at the corners of her lips.

"This," I said, holding out the diary.

Grandmother gasped softly when she saw the little, brown book with a buckle locking it securely.

"Where did you find that?" my grandma asked in shock, wiping her hands on a towel and gently taking the diary from my hands.

The look on Grandmother's face was both happy and sad, a look I didn't see from her that often. I *did* see it at times, though.

"I... found it in an abandoned bus—a bus filled with books. I visit there at times," I explained truthfully.

Grandmother's eyes filled with tears, which instantly made me concerned. I know I'm not really supposed to talk about my parents, and this *was* my mother's diary...

Grandmother looked at me with teary eyes and smiled gently. I could tell by the look on her face that she knew something I didn't. She handed me a kitchen knife, signaling for me to start cutting potatoes.

"That school bus drove your mother to her school, Lydia," explained Grandmother.

I sucked in my breath, the knife *almost* slipping from my hands by accident.

So, the bus is connected to all this...

"What... happened?" I asked in a small voice since this was obviously a very sensitive subject.

Grandmother patted my hand reassuringly.

"Your mother, Liliana, went to the same school that you go to now," Grandmother explained.

I nodded slowly.

"And… when she was in seventh grade…" My grandma trailed off and seemed to be having trouble with what she was to say next. Finally, she said in a low voice, "the school was robbed."

I gasped, looking at Grandmother with wide eyes. "What! Why would someone steal from a school?"

"I'm still not fully sure why," Grandmother replied.

I thought the school would have been safe enough to stop someone from breaking in. Frowning, I nodded for my grandmother to continue.

"The robbers—there were two—filled one of the school buses full of books. The strange thing is… not all of them were textbooks for subjects such as math and history. Nearly all of them were fiction. They weren't even from that school! Perplexing, isn't it? No one is sure where the fiction books came from."

I chewed my lip in thought. "How come the bus is still not at the school?"

"Well, the school buses at the school were already very old. The town had it in the newspapers about the books, but no one ever claimed them. The bus was at a gas station when it was found."

I was trying to take everything in, which was a little hard. I hadn't been expecting a story like *this*. It felt like my head was spinning!

Grandmother cleared her throat. "One day, it vanished. As years went by, people began to forget about the bus. *I* forgot about it. However, there was one person that must have never forgotten."

"Who?" I asked.

"Your mother," Grandmother told me gently. "It explains why her diary was in the bus."

I nodded. "That makes sense…"

Grandmother smiled a little. "However, I never knew that *you* found it. You and your mother really are alike, Lydia."

That made me grin.

* * *

Grandmother and I had finished dinner a few hours ago, and now I was pulling back the covers of my bed since tomorrow was a school day and I had to get up early.

I whistled for Charity to come in, and she obeyed, sprinting to my room. I then commanded her to lie down in her dog bed, which was in a corner of my room.

I was wearing some warm, turquoise-colored, flannel pajamas, the kind that button down the front of the shirt.

I turned off the ceiling light, so that only my lamp was on, and then climbed into bed.

My bedroom is painted white and turquoise. On the walls are starfish decorations and multiple drawings of sea creatures. The drawings are mostly whales since I *love* whales, just like my father did.

Father used to work at an aquarium. In my room, I also have a small, orange desk, which has a tank of fish on top and a white dresser. Plus, there is also an orange nightstand, with some books, a small flashlight (for late-night reading), and my seahorse alarm clock. My bed has a turquoise-, hot-pink-, and sea-green-colored comforter.

Grabbing one of the books on my nightstand, I tried to focus on the words. I read at night to help me get sleepy.

I couldn't focus on the story, however—even though it was about sea creatures! My mind kept wandering back to what Grandmother told me about the bus, then to Mom, then to Dad.

Turning off my lava lamp and closing my book, I couldn't push the thought out of my mind that a clue was missing…

* * *

"Kodiak Nobleman!"

I turned my head to the left side of my math classroom, only to see one of my best friends, Kodiak—or better known as Cody—spacing out during the math lesson. He was staring out the window.

Cody tore his hazel eyes away from the window, giving his attention to the teacher: Miss Paris Caden.

Miss Caden was a very pretty teacher in her mid-twenties, with long, dirty-blonde hair styled in big curls. She was tall, and her eyes were dark green. She almost always had a warm smile on her face. I instantly liked her as my teacher, and so did my friends! However, math wasn't one of Cody's best subjects, so he must have tuned out *again.* Miss Caden was kind but firm. Good qualities in a teacher, I suppose.

"Sorry, ma'am," Cody said to the teacher, his eyes gazing down at his desk and the papers that were atop it. Hearing some of the kids in the rows behind him snicker, I couldn't help but feel sorry for my friend.

Miss Caden nodded. "I was asking you if you could answer this problem here on the board."

Cody looked at the math question Miss Caden was pointing to with her pointer and then looked down at the paper on his desk. At last, he looked back up at the teacher and shook his head a little. "No, ma'am, I can't."

Some of the kids in the back snickered even more until Miss Caden silenced them.

The girl sitting next to me—who had long, sandy-brown curls in a high ponytail, and blue eyes—shot her left hand up.

"Yes, Felicia?" asked the teacher.

Felicia Blackwood was the name of the girl sitting on my right side. She is my other best friend, but Cody and I usually call her Fay as a nickname.

"The answer is 128," said Fay promptly.

Miss Caden smiled. "Well done, Felicia."

Fay beamed. "Thank you, Miss Caden."

Miss Caden quickly told us what we'd need to have done for tomorrow. She finished just in time before the bell went off and all the kids packed away their possessions, filing out of the classroom.

As I slung my backpack over my shoulder, and Fay did the same with her pink backpack trimmed in white lace, Cody nearly sprinted over to us.

"Hey, Cody," I said. "What's up?"

Cody grinned brightly. "Well, Dad and Mom bought a new stallion that you *need* to see!"

I grinned back. "They did? Cool! What breed?"

Cody lived on a ranch, to which Felicia and I went over quite frequently.

"A Thoroughbred!" Cody chirped excitedly. "And he's mine, too! I'll be in complete charge of him!"

Cody, Fay, and I were walking to the lunchroom as we talked.

"What color? Have you named him?" Fay asked enthusiastically.

Cody nodded yes. "He's solid black! I named him Nightfall."

"Oh, that's fitting!" I said with a laugh as the three of us walked down the hallway.

Shifting his plain, light-brown-colored, leather backpack over his shoulder, Cody snorted. "True."

I debated if I should tell my friends about the secret in the bus, or if I should keep it to myself.

I wasn't sure that I was really ready to tell my two friends about the bus, or the secret, even if they were my best friends.

"So, do you think that'd work, Lia?" asked Kodiak. Lia is *my* nickname.

I blinked. "Sorry, what? I kind of spaced out."

Fay smiled. "He asked if it'd work for you and me to come see Nightfall after school tomorrow."

"Oh, that'd be amazing! I'll ask my grandmother," I replied.

"And I'll ask my parents if I can go," Fay said with a smirk.

Cody nodded as we walked into the lunchroom. "Sounds like a plan then!"

* * *

When the final bell for the day rang out, I bid both my friends farewell and hurried down the sidewalks. I wanted to go to the bus again!

Normally, I'd go home first, so that I could take Charity with me. Today, however, I wanted to get to the bus as soon as possible.

The weather was cool, so I slowed down only for a brief moment to pull my denim jacket on over my gray- and navy-blue-striped sweater.

The bronze buckles on my dark-brown boots clicked merrily as I ran. My boots were the tall kind, not ankle boots. I was wearing a just-below-the-knee, navy-blue, corduroy skirt, which had pleats, along with gray leggings. I also had on the navy hat I wore yesterday.

As I recognized the familiar turn that led to the alley, I slowed down.

Glancing over my shoulder, I quickly snuck into the hidden place.

I smiled to myself as I opened up the door to the bus carefully, remembering what happened yesterday with the books tumbling out and all.

If I'd stack the books neatly, I could probably make my hideout into a library also, and I could walk in. I really should consider that…

Deciding that I wanted to shield myself from the cold a little, plus that it'd be nice to go into the bus, rather than sit on the bus step, I cleared some of the books out of the way. It wasn't hard, other than that every once and a while one would fall and tumble out, followed by a few others, making me have to catch them all.

Suddenly, I heard a loud thud!

I was startled out of my skin, making me get tangled up in the books piled by my legs.

Before I could fall, I regained my balance, setting down the several books I was holding.

When I looked out of the bus, I was met with the surprised stare of Felicia Blackwood and the unfortunate sight of Kodiak Nobleman on top of the dirt, his hands having caught him from slamming headfirst onto the ground.

"Oops," said Cody sheepishly. Knowing him, he must have tripped over his own two feet.

"So… this is where you've been going after school so often," said Felicia, getting over the shock and apparently assuming Cody was fine. (She also ignored the fact that Cody had totally blown their cover.)

"Whoa…" Cody breathed. "Why didn't you tell us about your secret headquarters?"

That made me laugh aloud.

"Well…" I began, looking down a little, "I—"

"Because," Fay gently told Cody for me, "she wanted it as her *own* secret."

I gave Fay a grateful smile. "That's true."

Cody said an, "Oh, that makes sense, I guess," and then rose to his feet, brushing the dust off his light-blue jeans.

"Sorry about deciding to follow you. I understand if you didn't want us to," Fay began. "We were *really* curious, though."

I nodded. "It's okay. How'd you guys know, though?"

"Well, I didn't realize it," replied Cody. "Fay did."

"You've been leaving very quickly after school lately, without taking time to talk. I told Cody about it, and we decided we should check and make sure everything was okay," Fay explained.

"I see. Well, thanks for looking out for me. Everything's fine. I just discovered this place a while back, you know. It's full of books," I told my two friends, grinning.

"Sweet!" Cody cheered excitedly. He instantly went over to the bus and started sorting through the books.

"Do you know anything about how this bus got here?" Fay asked me, staring at the yellow school bus.

The flashback of my conversation with my grandmother flashed through my mind.

"Yes, I do," I replied, wondering if I wanted to tell them what I learned, or just leave it at that.

Fay looked at me with an expression eager to find out. However, as if reading my thoughts, she said, "You don't have to say if you don't want to."

I smiled a little. What was I thinking, anyway? These were my best friends! I could *totally* trust them not to tell all of Wilsonville.

"Well," I began, "it turns out that this bus used to be owned by the school we go to."

Cody stopped looking at one of the books about horses and looked up at me with curiosity.

"Why doesn't our school still own it?" he asked.

I quickly started explaining about how the school was robbed and then how the bus was found at a gas station, where it disappeared, only for my mother and later me, to find it. I also added about finding Mom's diary yesterday. Fay took everything in with bright and alert eyes.

"Like mother, like daughter…" Fay muttered under her breath, a smile tugging at the corners of her lips.

Cody tapped the bus's doorway with his finger in thought. "I wonder why it ended up here..."

I shrugged. "No clue."

"Well," Fay began, trying to piece everything together, although this mystery wasn't a simple puzzle, "it could be *anything*. Since *nobody* goes here, not even the *alley cats,* it'd be a perfect spot to get the bus out of the way. Or..." Fay trailed off.

"Or what?" Cody asked, raising an eyebrow.

"Or it'd be the perfect spot to *hide* it," replied Fay.

I chewed my lip in thought. "Why would someone hide the bus?"

Fay tossed her hand in the air. "Just a thought. Perhaps it's something else."

I noticed my sandy-haired friend looked a little uneasy, all of a sudden.

"What's the matter?" I said.

"Are you sure we should even be here?" Fay asked, looking over her shoulder.

Cody cocked his head to the side a little. "Why wouldn't we be able to be here?" he questioned.

Fay then whispered in a low voice, "Suppose that someone *does* come through this alley?"

I felt a sinking feeling in my stomach.

Fay does have a point. But then again...

"I don't suppose they would. Not even the alley cats come here. Remember?" I asked.

"But *you* did," Fay replied.

I opened my mouth to reply but then closed it, unsure of what to say.

Finally, after a moment to gather my thoughts, I said: "I want to be here. I think there could be clues on how my parents died. Remember how after their death, Grandmother would never tell me what happened? I'm not sure even *she* knows."

Now it was Fay's turn to be unsure how to reply. She thought for a moment, leaving Cody and me in suspense. At last, she sighed and said, "I see what you mean. Also, it would be good to know what happened. For all we know, if it was a person who caused their deaths…" She paused some, as if a little worried about what to say. She then whispered, "they could still be on the loose."

Cody jumped up from where he had been sitting on the bus steps.

"You think *murderers* are out and about?" he shouted a little louder than intended.

I put a finger to my lips with a sympathetic smile. Glancing behind myself I saw a woman going into a shop, but she didn't seem to hear Cody's yell.

Cody sheepishly quieted down.

"It's all right," I said. Fay nodded.

"Thanks," Cody replied. "I've got to go home, but we'll talk about this tomorrow. I've got chores, you know. Oh, and Lia, when you come to the house tomorrow, assuming your grandmother lets you, maybe you should bring the diary?"

I nodded. "That'd be fine. I'll bring it."

Fay picked up her pink backpack that she had set down earlier. "Also, we'll need to look for clues. We're going to need evidence. Can you collect *any* possible info that might be helpful as well?" she asked me.

I nodded again. "Yeah, I'll try and see what I can do."

"Sounds good," Cody told us, about to put away the book he had been reading earlier. I stopped him, however.

"You can take it home if you want, Code," I said.

Cody grinned, despite the fact we were just talking about there possibly being a murderer on the loose. "Oh, all right! Thanks, Lia!"

"As for now, I'll see you both tomorrow. I forgot I simply must go home and help my mother. Father is having a couple of people from his job over for dinner tonight, and I have got to help prepare," explained Fay quickly, about to start walking to her house.

"Sure thing. Catch ya later, Fay!" Cody chirped.

I said goodbye to both my friends and then headed to my house, wondering just what possibly dangerous idea my friends and I had gotten ourselves into, all because of a diary.

Away from the Stables
Chapter 3

I got permission from my grandmother to go to
Cody's house today. The school day seemed to
take forever, but at last, it finally ended.

I told Cody and Fay I was going to my house
really quickly so that I could get my stuff and bring
Charity. Fay was going to bring her own dog,
Gracie. Gracie is small and fluffy, with curly, white
fur. She *loves* to get her ears scratched.

I hurried to my home quickly. When I got close,
I sprinted and then ran up the driveway. Taking only

a moment to wipe my feet, I swung open the door, barging through.

I made a mad dash to my bedroom, shouting, "I'm home!"

When I got to my bedroom in what seemed three seconds flat, I grabbed my cross-body leather bag and carefully put in the diary. Shoving a few papers into my bag, which matched my backpack, I then rushed out of my room.

I hurried into the kitchen, seeing my grandma getting ready to cook meatloaf.

"Hey, Grandmother!" I yelled.

Grandmother cracked a smile. "Hello to you too."

Charity had been sitting at Grandmother's feet, but she got up to greet me.

"You ready to go, girl?" I asked, running my fingers through Charity's fur and breathing in her cute puppy scent.

My dog wagged her tail happily and barked, making me laugh aloud.

"I'll take that as a yes," I said, grinning.

I hugged Grandmother goodbye and then grabbed Charity's blue- and orange-striped collar as well as her matching leash by the front door.

Opening the door, Charity and I left the house, and we hurried down the sidewalks. A chilly wind blew, making the leaves on the trees rustle.

I was wearing a black, long-sleeved shirt and a short-sleeved, dark-blue jean shirt over it. I was also wearing dark-blue jeans since I'd likely ride a horse or two at Cody's house. I had my boots on that I wore the day before, and my hair was in a simple braid.

Sometimes I ride my bicycle to Cody's, but on this day, I just decided to walk.

Despite the chill in the air, I wasn't miserably cold. The walking kept me warm.

I was able to get to Cody's house fairly fast. Upon seeing Gracie (who was dressed in a pink tutu) and Cody's family's dogs—Blue, Arrow, and Gopher—in the backyard, I let Charity play with them. Blue is a collie, Arrow is an Australian cattle dog, and Gopher is a corgi.

I gave each of the dogs a pat on the head, and the dogs wagged their tails happily in response.

Since Cody is one of my best friends, I don't bother to knock before walking into his house; I just walk right in.

I had seen Fay's bike parked outside, so I knew she must have gotten here before me.

I could hear Cody and Fay talking nearby, so I instantly slipped off my boots and followed their voices.

Cody's house is elegant in a western way. The floors are wooden, and the carpet is a chocolate-brown color with a very soft texture. The couches are made of leather, and there are several cowhide rugs, including one in the living room and one in the dining room. Throughout the house, there are multiple chandeliers made with antlers, and there are paintings of cattle and roosters and horses, as well as family photos. There is also an enormous brick fireplace, which cheerfully cracks.

In the kitchen are red- and white-checkered curtains as well as some potted plants of different shapes and sizes.

Cody's father was at work, but his mother was home.

"Hi, Mrs. Nobleman!" I chirped as I walked into the kitchen.

Cody's mother smiled warmly. She was a nice woman, about average in height, with honey-blonde hair and brown eyes. Her husband, Mr. Nobleman, has ginger-red hair and green eyes, so I suppose Cody is a perfect mix of his parents.

"Hello, Lydia," replied Mrs. Nobleman, giving me a hug which I happily hugged back to. "Cody and Felicia are eating some coleslaw up in his room. There's a bowl for you too."

"Thanks!" I replied. My friends and I all love coleslaw, and Mrs. Nobleman's coleslaw is the best ever! Cody, Fay, and I almost always have some at Cody's house.

Cody's parents are the closest thing to parents I've got due to my own mother and father passing away. Mr. and Mrs. Nobleman are very kind. I always feel comfortable around them. Nothing can replace my mom and dad, though.

I headed straight to Cody's room, which is upstairs. I didn't bother to hold onto the beautifully carved wooden rail as I sprinted up.

When I reached Cody's room, I saw him and Fay sitting cross-legged on the floor, eating some coleslaw as a snack. They were also looking over some math homework.

Cody's room has a smooth, dark-colored, wooden floor, with a cowhide rug in the center. His walls are painted white, and there are bronze horseshoe decorations hung up. His bedframe is sturdy and made of wood, with a colorful quilt on top. When he isn't wearing it, Cody's black cowboy hat is tilted slightly on one of the bedframe posts. There is a wooden nightstand by his bed, which has a horseshoe alarm clock on top and several books about horses and astronomy. The one horse book I let him take home yesterday was put on the very top of the stack. A horse calendar is on the wall, and a horse painting that he painted himself. Cody's the artist among us.

"Hi guys," I said, sitting down next to my friends.

Cody waved. "Long time no see."

"Hey, Lia," said Fay.

Taking off my cross-body bag, I smiled. "I gathered some info as well as the diary."

"Cool!" Cody said as I opened my bag and pulled out the diary.

"This," I began, "is the diary."

Fay eyed it and then said, "May I see?"

I nodded, putting the diary gently in her hands.

Carefully opening the diary, Fay flipped through the pages. Cody and I looked over her shoulder.

"Perhaps there are clues in the diary?" Fay considered.

I shrugged. "I'm not sure. Could be."

Then, I reached into my bag and pulled out some papers. "I also found my mother and father's medical records. It took some effort, but I found them in my grandmother's room this morning, before school. She must have gotten them after mom and dad died."

I handed the records to Cody, and he studied them in silence.

I sighed. "I thought I might be able to find some other records, too, but I couldn't find anything."

Fay cleared her throat, setting down the diary. "You know... this is still good. It might prove useful."

I nodded. "And I'll keep looking."

Fay furrowed her eyebrow in thought. "Maybe if... Lia, do you know some people that your parents grew up with? We could try to gather information from them."

"That's a good idea," Cody said, grinning a little.

I grinned too. "It is indeed. Some of their friends still live here. How about we try to visit them?"

"Sounds good to me," Fay said.

Cody nodded in agreement, grinning goofily as he munched on a bit of coleslaw. "Yeah! We could spilt up and gather as much info as possible."

It felt good to have a plan that would possibly lead us one step closer to finding out about Mom and Dad.

"Thanks, guys," I told my two best friends.

"No problem," said Cody.

Fay nodded. "Agreed."

Another thought occurred to me. "When should we go out and search?"

Fay sighed. "I can't tomorrow."

"Me neither," said Cody.

I laughed a little. "Neither can I. Maybe on Saturday?"

Fay and Cody thought for a moment.

Brightening, Fay said, "Sure, that'd work."

"Same here!" chirped Cody.

"Great!" I replied.

Fay looked as if she was already thinking the details through. "How about we meet up by the bus on Saturday morning? I'll bring a map of the neighborhood, and we'll check and see who will cover where."

"Sharp as a tack, Fay!" Cody said with a laugh.

I nodded to say I agreed with Cody. "You're brilliant!"

Felicia just shrugged it off modestly, although I could see a little smile tug at the corners of her lips.

"Anyway, I'm glad we've got a plan," she said.

"Me too," I replied.

"Mm-hmm," Cody mumbled, apparently zoning out a little. He was likely thinking about showing us the horses.

"Should we see the stallion now?" Fay asked, looking at me with a smirk. After all, that *was* why we were originally coming here!

Cody instantly beamed. "Want to go see?" he asked. His hazel eyes were literally sparkling.

I laughed. "Sure!"

* * *

So that was how I found myself perched on a wooden fence.

Cody *had* been just going to *show* me and Fay the horse, but soon he was hopping up onto the saddle and riding all around the ranch. It was kind of amusing, to be honest.

Fay was leaning next to me on the fence.

"Do you suppose he'll ever let us ride?" asked Fay.

I shrugged. "At this point, who knows?"

We literally just watched Cody ride around for several minutes before he rode over to us at last, purposely tipping his cowboy hat to make us laugh.

Now that Cody had finally *slowed down,* Fay and I could get a good look at his horse, Nightfall.

Nightfall was tall and of a glossy black color seeming to have a deep-blue glow in the light. His mane was soft and sleek.

I hopped off the fence and pulled some long grass out of the ground. I then held out my hand to Nightfall. The stallion nestled his velvety muzzle into my hand. His rough tongue licked out the grass as he snorted a little. I snickered.

"He's a goose!" I said.

"No, he's not!" Cody replied with a grin. "He's a horse."

Fay smirked a little. "How tall is he?"

"Seventeen hands," Cody answered simply.

I rose an eyebrow, impressed. "That's tall!"

Felicia, quite perplexed, mused, "Seventeen *hands?* Why, don't you mean feet?"

"If that were the case, Fay, he'd be really tall!" Cody responded with glee, obviously delighted he knew more about horses than Felicia.

"What would that be in the metric system?" I asked with a laugh.

Cody gave a facial expression somewhere between a grin and a smirk and then tilted his head over to the stables.

"Do you guys want to go ride too?" he asked.

Fay and I nodded yes.

I followed Cody and Fay over to the stables and smiled as I saw the rows of horses all lined up.

Cody's older brother, Ryker, was also in the stables, brushing a gray mare named Trigger. Quite a cowboy-sounding name.

Ryker was older than Cody by a few years—four to be exact, which set him at sixteen years old. He was quite a tall teenager—wiry, even. Both brothers looked pretty different when it came to their hair and eye colors, though. Ryker had blue eyes and dark-brown hair, but Cody had strawberry-blond hair and hazel eyes. One of the similarities, however, was that both brothers had freckles.

Cody grinned at his older sibling. "What's up, Pitchfork?"

Pitchfork is a nickname that Cody gave Ryker due to Ryker being thin but strong. Cody prefers to use the word *scrawny* rather than thin, but that's a little extreme to describe Ryker. Actually, it's really extreme.

Ryker snorted. He took the nickname well. "Not much, Cross Eyes."

Cross Eyes was Ryker's nickname for Cody. I honestly have *no* idea how it started. Fay knows as much about it as I do. If you ask Cody, he will always reply with a grin, never really answering.

Felicia was petting a white stallion who was named Cupid.

Ryker grinned. "Are you guys going riding?"

Cody nodded. "Yup."

"Well," Ryker began, grin growing. "Don't trip on your spurs like you did *last* time."

"That only happened once!" Cody retorted in a huff.

Okay, I'm not going to lie. Cody trips on nearly *everything.* It's rather funny, to be honest. How he managed to trip on spurs, I have no clue.

Fay giggled a little as Ryker reminded his brother that there were actually *two* times Cody tripped on spurs.

Cody crossed his arms over his chest and stormed out of the stable, yelling, "Come on, girls, let's go!"

I know Cody is only pretending to be furious. He and Ryker tease each other every day, it seems.

"See you later, Rhys," I said. (Rhys is Ryker's nickname.)

Ryker waved back. "Later!"

I grabbed a rope and gently led the brown mare *I* had chosen, who's called Buttercup, away from the stables.

ANOTHER CLUE
Chapter 4

The rest of the week flew by quickly, and Saturday rolled around.

I was riding my simple, blue bicycle, which has silver streamers on the handlebars, over to the bus. After all, this was the day my friends and I planned to get info about Mom and Dad—assuming we could.

Charity was following me on the sidewalks. She was barking happily. I didn't have her on a leash. Because Wilsonville is so small, no one cares whether dogs are on leashes.

It was cloudy out and a little chilly.

When I reached the alley, I parked my bike and sat on the bus steps. Cody and Fay weren't there yet, so it was just Charity and me.

The alley was dark and a little creepy. It has no pavement, only dirt and weeds, due to Wilsonville being such a small place.

I picked up a book and began reading, hoping I could pass the time. (I should have brought a watch.)

Charity was lying at my feet.

The whole town seemed quiet this morning. Of course, this makes sense because there is scarcely *any* commotion in Wilsonville. There never seems to be much traffic. I like how peaceful it is, to be honest. Big cities are too busy and noisy. Well, they're too big to *live* in, but they're nice to visit.

Suddenly, I heard a noise. I turned my head up to look, Charity's ears shooting straight into the air.

I saw Fay riding over on her pale-pink bicycle. Her bicycle had silver streamers on the handlebars, like my streamers, and her wheels were white. There was also a white basket on the front, which Gracie was riding in.

"Hi!" I said as Fay slowed down and then stopped.

Fay got off her bike and waved. "Hi, Lia. How's it going?"

"Good, except for *that*," I replied, pointing up at the clouds which were looking a little darker than they had been.

Fay grabbed Gracie out of the basket on the bike and looked up at the clouds.

"You're right, Lia," stated Fay. "It looks like it will possibly storm."

I hoped that wouldn't be the case, considering we'd have to postpone our search.

"Where's Cody?" I asked, changing the subject.

Shrugging, Fay responded, "Who knows?"

"I really shouldn't be shocked," I said with a laugh. "Cody's usually late."

Fay smirked. "That's true. Remember how he was late to Ryker's birthday party before?"

"Yes!" I shouted, thinking back to the memory. "It took him thirty minutes to finally show up!"

Sure, Cody wasn't *always* late, but he *did* tend to forget things and dates.

Grinning, Fay set down Gracie and said, "I brought the map."

She handed it to me, and I unfolded it.

"This will work great," I replied, scanning the map.

Charity and Gracie were running around the alley, having a good time.

About five minutes later, I tore my eyes away from watching the dogs play because I heard someone shout, "I'm here!"

Cody rode over to us at a recklessly high speed. I couldn't help wondering how he didn't crash.

He was just a few feet away from us, making us step out of the way as he abruptly stopped.

Cody's dog, Gopher, ran into the alleyway, barking.

"Sorry I'm late!" shouted Cody.

I nodded. "It's all right. We weren't waiting very long."

Fay smirked. Teasingly, she said, "Now that you're *finally* here, we can go over the plan."

I grinned because Cody had arrived only about five minutes after Fay.

Cody playfully rolled his eyes and waited for Felicia to explain our strategy.

Fay took in a deep breath. "Okay, so first off, here's the map of the neighborhood."

"All right," said Cody.

Fay then used her finger to divide the map into three sections. "Cody, you'll take the west part of town, see? Lia will take the center, and I'll take the east."

Kodiak nodded. "Makes sense so far."

"Good," Fay said. "We'll knock on the doors. If someone is home, we'll ask them about Lia's mother and father. If they don't know anything, then we'll try the next house."

"What if they're not home?" Cody asked.

"Then we won't ask them," Fay replied with a snicker.

I laughed aloud. I was feeling a little excited and nervous. It'd be great if I could find a clue about Mom and Dad, but... at the same time, I still felt anxious about *what* I could learn.

Looking back at the map, Fay then tapped an area in the center, about two thirds up the map. "This is where we are. Let's all try to get back to this spot in an hour, okay? Does that sound good?"

"That'd be fine," I replied.

Cody grinned and nodded.

Felicia beamed. "Good! Then I'll see you guys soon!"

* * *

I was pedaling my bike to my first stop. Charity was following alongside me, happily barking.

Glancing up, I saw that the clouds were growing darker. I hoped it wouldn't rain.

The streets were pretty quiet right now. There were just a few young children, first- or second-graders, playing hopscotch. They waved to me; I waved back.

The first house I was going to was a doctor's house—Doctor Edwin Layton's house. He was polite, friendly, and a little bald. Not fully bald, just a little bald. The hair he had was very dark, almost black, and then it faded out into gray.

Doctor Layton had been living here for years, but his clinic was about fifteen miles away in a town called Cambridge. My mother used to work for him because Mom was a nurse.

I hoped Doctor Layton would know some useful information.

I rode close to his house, then parked my bike, kicking the kickstand into place. One thing I knew was that Doctor Layton loved dogs. He'd definitely want to see Charity.

Charity and I made our way to the doctor's front door, where I rang the doorbell, setting the simple and clear chime off.

A brief moment passed by until I heard the doorknob turn. The door opened, and in the doorway stood Mr. Layton.

The kind doctor smiled and said, "Well hello, Lydia! Come in."

I smiled back. "Hi, Doctor Layton. Sorry for showing up on short notice."

"It's no trouble, child. What brings you by on this cloudy day? I believe it is going to rain!"

Walking into the house, I nodded. "That's what I've been thinking. The clouds *are* rather dark."

"Aye," Doctor Layton replied.

I picked up Charity so that Doctor Layton could easily greet her.

"Again, sorry to arrive on short notice," I apologized.

"No trouble at all! You're such pleasant company. Is everything well? Is anyone sick?" asked the doctor, petting my dog.

I shook my head. "Oh, no, it's not that at all; everyone's healthy. I came over to ask a question, actually, if you don't mind."

"I don't mind at all. What might it be, Lydia?" Doctor Layton inquired, sitting down on one of the couches.

I sat down on one across from him.

"Well… I was wondering if you knew anything about… the cause of my parents'… death…"

Doctor Layton's eyes widened a little.

"Why are you asking this?" he inquired softly.

I gave the doctor an apologetic look. "Sorry, I know it's a very unexpected question. It's just that it's been three years now, and I still haven't found out who or what did it."

The doctor nodded. "I understand."

Charity lay down next to me on the couch. Doctor Layton didn't mind.

"Well," the doctor began softly, "I'm not entirely sure about the whole story. I did hear some of what happened, however."

"Even a little information would help!" I replied.

"Of course," agreed the doctor.

I ran my fingers through Charity's fur as I waited a moment for Doctor Layton to start. Doctor Layton cleared his throat a little awkwardly.

"I heard it had been a late night. Your father was at the aquarium he had worked at."

I nodded soberly, taking in this small piece of information.

Doctor Layton paused a moment, closing his eyes as if to help him remember what he had heard.

"On that particular night, Lydia, most of the workers had gone home. I'm not entirely sure who was there and who wasn't. I do know one thing, though. Your father was there, and your mother was there too."

"Why was Mom there?" I asked. I had been at Fay's house for a sleepover the night Dad and Mom died. Fay and I were already dozing off when Mrs. Blackwood came in. She somehow broke the news to us. We didn't sleep at all that night.

Shrugging, Doctor Layton replied, "I don't know why your mother was at the aquarium. I'm sorry."

"It's okay," I responded and waited for the doctor to continue.

"I never fully heard what happened, but... it's clear that your mother and father weren't the only ones at that aquarium. Sorry, Lydia. That's all I know," finished Doctor Layton.

Nodding, I said, "Thank you for your time, Doctor. I appreciate it. I'm another step closer to finding out what happened that night."

I felt glad to know more but heartsick at the same time.

"I'm happy I could help you out, Lydia," responded Doctor Layton with a smile.

However, one look out the window and the doctor exclaimed, "Why, Lydia! It looks like it will rain any minute. Won't your grandmother worry?"

I looked outside, and I knew Doctor Layton was right. The storm clouds were dark and thick in the sky.

"You're right, Doctor. I've got to see my friends! We met up this morning to go find out clues, you see. We split up. I don't think *Cody* would even continue the search when the sky looks like *this*."

"You'd best go see them in that case," Doctor Layton replied. "Perhaps you can beat the race against the rain!"

"I'll try to. Thanks again!" I shouted, Charity and I already on our way out the door.

* * *

Thankfully, it hadn't started to rain just then. However, I felt it would start to sprinkle any minute. Once it'd start sprinkling, it'd start pouring, and once it'd start pouring, I'd be sopping wet. Grandmother would worry I'd catch a cold.

I knew my way around Wilsonville, and I especially knew the way to the abandoned bus. After all, I do go there a *lot*. Obviously, I would be able to reach the alley quite fast.

As I quickly pedaled my bicycle, I frequently glanced at the clouds. Charity was able to keep up with me. She's a frisky pup.

I certainly didn't want to stop. I didn't want to slow down.

A loud roar of thunder had me wondering how much longer it'd be until the downpour. If it started to rain right now, I'd have to slow down so I wouldn't crash.

Thunder roared again, and I started to pedal even faster.

Minutes ticked by. I counted the seconds between each lightning strike in my head.

I was riding so fast.

Maybe I should consider being in a bike race.

I let out a short laugh, despite the fact I was breathing heavy and my heart was pounding in my chest.

I was getting close.

Thunder sounded again. I could see there was already a storm in the distance.

At last, I saw the alley. I made a slightly reckless turn and abruptly jolted my ride to a halt.

"Phew!" I yelled in exhaustion. "I beat the rain."

At that moment, Felicia came riding up. She was riding fast, but not as fast or reckless as I had been.

I waved. "Hey!"

"Hi!" Fay shouted back, stopping her bike. "Have you seen Cody?"

"No, not yet," I replied, breathing hard from my ride.

Fay wiped the sweat away from her forehead. "Surely he's still not—"

"I'm here!" yelled a breathless voice.

Fay and I turned to see Kodiak zoom over to us on his bike. He entered the alley even more recklessly than I had moments earlier. Cody nearly crashed but managed to stop himself just in time.

"Guess I'm a little late," said the strawberry-blond boy.

"Just a little," I reassured.

"Yeah, we just got here," Fay added.

I glanced up at the clouds again.

"Want to come to my house? We can tell each other about our searches, and you know my house isn't far. It looks like it's going to rain soon," I said.

Fay nodded. "I agree. And sure, I'd like to come over."

"Me too," Cody said with a grin.

Just then, I saw some lightning.

"In that case, we'd better get going right now," I replied, pointing to the sky.

* * *

We had been just minutes away from my house when it started sprinkling. The large drops had landed on the concrete with a plop. Soon, more and more drops had plopped on the ground. Then it started pouring. Thankfully, we made it to my house just when the downpour started, so we weren't very wet. Now, Cody, Fay, and I were sitting on the couch drinking strawberry milk while the fireplace crackled cheerfully.

I explained the news I had learned while at Doctor Layton's house.

Fay took everything in, and now she was deep in thought.

Cody sighed, also thinking. "This is kind of confusing."

Nodding, Fay said, "It really is a mystery. I was talking to Mrs. Williams, and she hadn't known anything, but her neighbor Mrs. Norwood did know. Mrs. Norwood, like Mr. Layton, told me that whatever had happened that night happened at the aquarium."

Cody took a sip of his strawberry milk. "I asked Mr. Smith if he had known anything, but he didn't, and neither did Mrs. Carleton."

I nodded and rose to my feet, leaving for the kitchen so I could rinse my glass. My friends followed me.

"Overall," began Felicia, "I'd say the search went pretty well."

"Yeah," I replied, rinsing my glass and putting it in the sink. As I turned to go, however, I noticed a large drop of water fall down right next to me.

Cody raised an eyebrow and looked up at the ceiling. "Does your ceiling always do that?"

I shook my head. "No."

Fay reached for a pie pan in the cabinet, and she quickly put it on the ground so that the water would fall into the pan instead of on the floor.

"There," she said.

I looked back up at the ceiling and then at the water falling into the pie pan. "Thanks, Fay."

"No problem."

"Should we see why your ceiling is leaking, Lia?" asked Cody.

"Sure, that'd probably be a good idea," I said with a laugh.

The three of us then made our way up to my attic.

The attic was simple. Its floor and walls were wooden. The floor itself creaked. It was a little dark in the attic because there were only four small windows. There was a light bulb that would turn on if you pulled the long chain attached to it, but it was a little defective, often flickering on and off. The cobwebs on the walls along with old furniture and other things gave the attic an eerie feeling. Tracing my finger on an old dresser, I looked at the thick coating of dust I removed.

Some water was leaking through the roof. Cody pointed to it.

"Maybe some of your shingles got blown off during the storm," he said. "That happened to our barn once."

I shrugged. Grinning a little, I replied, "Could be. Nice thinking."

Cody grinned back but then looked over at some big, old-looking thing nearby. It was hard to see in the faint lighting.

"What's that?" Cody asked.

I followed his gaze. "It looks like an old, wooden chest. I don't know why it's up here, though."

Walking over to it, I knelt down. The wooden chest had some pretty carvings on it, and the wood was smooth and glossy.

My friends came to look at it too.

Felicia brushed some dust off the wooden chest, making Cody sneeze.

All of us were curious about what could possibly be inside.

"On three?" Fay asked.

Cody and I nodded.

Fay grinned. "One… two… three!"

She pushed the lid up, and we looked at the single possession inside the chest with wonder.

I carefully pulled out the object.

Cody tilted his head.

"Is it… a book?" he asked.

"Something like that," I replied.

The book was made of dark-red leather, with a buckle on the side. It was plain, except for the wavy designs outlining it.

Setting the book on my lap, I carefully opened it. Inside were various sketches, pictures, and writings, and they were all about sea creatures!

Fay looked at the book, perplexed. "Is this a journal of your father's, perhaps?"

Shrugging, I said, "Maybe."

I carefully turned the pages, looking at the things written and drawn all over. Then, turning to the very front of the book, I stared at the handwriting written on the top left corner: *Seth Arlington.* That was Father's name!

Thunder boomed extremely loudly, making my friends and me jump.

Handing the book to Cody, I gave him a chance to read.

"This *must* have been your dad's journal or something," Cody told me.

"Yeah," I replied. "It could be another clue!"

Cody then handed the book to Fay.

Fay flipped through the pages. "I wonder why it was in this huge wooden chest, all by itself, though."

"I don't know," I said, feeling a little confused.

As Fay handed the small journal back to me, something thin and light fell out of it and floated down to the floor.

Tilting my head, I gently picked up what had fallen.

It was just a simple piece of small, creamy-white paper. It had rough, ripped edges, as if someone carelessly ripped it out of a book.

I slowly turned the paper over in my hands.

"Look, guys," I said. "This paper has something drawn on it."

Cody and Fay stared at it with curiosity.

"What is it?" asked Cody.

I squinted since the lighting was dim.

"It's a whale from the aquarium in Ashland," I replied, smiling a little. "I remember Father had named him Orion. Orion had joined the aquarium just a week before Father and Mother died."

Back when my parents were alive, Father had been the manager of three aquariums: one in Scottsbluff, one in Wichita, and one in Ashland. Wilsonville is rather evenly spaced between them all, so it had been the perfect place for Father, Mother, and me to live.

Fay nodded solemnly and then asked gently, "Is Orion still at the aquarium?"

"Yes, I believe so," I replied. "He was there the last time I was at the aquarium, but that was a long time ago. It's been about six months, maybe longer..."

Cody smiled a little as if he had thought of an idea. "Maybe we could go visit him!" he chirped.

I laughed. "I'd like that. Maybe Grandmother will let me soon."

Tucking the small paper back into the journal, I decided I'd take the book to my room. Maybe, just maybe, this was another clue...

STRAⁿGER!
Chapter 5

Next week, I was in math class again.

Miss Caden was going through the lesson, holding a pointer. However, when I saw her point to some numbers on the board, a glitter caught my eye from a ring on Miss Caden's hand. That hadn't been there before.

Fay and I exchanged glances. She must have seen it too.

Whispering, Felicia said, "Did you see that? It's an *engagement* ring!"

My eyes widened, and I flashed Fay a grin.

"Really?" I whispered back a little louder than intended.

Miss Caden looked at us, obviously aware we were whispering. However, she seemed to be in a good mood, and she let us off the hook.

We looked over at Cody to see if he had noticed Miss Caden's ring, but he was starting to space out like he tends to do.

I looked back at the board and tried to pay attention. I was so excited about the discovery, though, that it was hard to study!

My mind kept wandering back and forth from the math lesson to Miss Caden's ring. But when I heard the door that led to the hallway open a crack, I tilted my head in wonder.

Slowly and quietly, as if not to disturb, the door opened all the way. In stepped a rather tall young man with light-brown hair and blue eyes. He was wearing a flannel shirt which was checkered, along with some pale-blue jeans, and boots. The western hat on his head made me almost sure he was a cowboy or a rancher.

The whole class stared with big eyes at the man. (Even Cody gave him his full attention.)

The young man looked at all of us for a moment and then looked over to Miss Caden.

"You forgot these," he said, handing Miss Caden some papers. I assumed they were for an upcoming test.

I hadn't seen this man before. He seemed to be in his mid-twenties. Considering I knew just about everyone in Wilsonville, I figured he must be new.

Miss Caden took the papers and smiled. "Oh, thank you!"

"You're welcome," replied the man, smiling back.

The whole class, myself included, seemed to be inspecting this brown-haired stranger like a hawk.

Finally, when no student could bear it any longer, Cody said bluntly, "Who are *you?*"

Half the class burst into a fit of giggles, and Miss Caden had to quiet them down.

"Children," began Miss Caden with a smile, "this is Uriah Harper."

There was a moment of silence as if we all wanted to greet him, but at the same time, we didn't know if we had the permission.

Miss Caden laughed. "You may say hello."

In unison, we all enthusiastically said, "Hello, Mr. Harper!"

Miss Caden then smiled a little more than she had a moment ago. "Uriah is also my fiancé."

I grinned. There was a round of cheers going around the room, but Miss Caden hushed everyone, saying, "We must let Mr. Harper get back to work, and we must also!"

Tipping his hat before leaving, Mr. Harper smiled and walked out the door.

Miss Caden turned back to the board, ready to continue the math lesson.

Despite the questions running through my head, I picked up my pencil and tried to devote my mind to arithmetic.

* * *

The school bell rang, and the kids in the class all began to rush out of the classroom, gathering up their papers and books and pencils.

Kodiak, Felicia, and I gathered up our stuff and then, before leaving, went to talk to Miss Caden.

"Need any help cleaning up?" I inquired. Besides, we had questions to ask!

"That would be lovely, Lydia. Thank you," replied Miss Caden with a smile.

Cody started straightening up the backrow chairs. The backrow students have a thing for moving their chairs crooked.

Fay beamed at our teacher. "Have you set a date yet?" she all but shouted enthusiastically.

Miss Caden laughed. "For the wedding?"

Fay nodded.

"Yes, Felicia. It's on the nineteenth of June," replied Miss Caden.

"What a lovely date," cheered Fay, "just hours before summer!"

Cody snorted in the background, and I laughed.

Miss Caden laughed too but said, "That's just what I was thinking, Felicia."

I liked the date too. My birthday is on June twelfth, so it would be just after I turned thirteen.

Fay then started rambling, eager to learn what she could about the wedding.

My friends and I straightened up the classroom with our teacher. Once the room was neat and tidy, we told Miss Caden goodbye, heading out to finish the rest of our school day.

* * *

"It's just so exciting!" chirped Fay as the three of us walked down the sidewalk. "About the wedding, I mean."

"Mm-hmm," Cody replied, a little out of it. He was obviously stressing over the math test we had coming up. Fay never has any problems with tests, it seems. She is always at the very top in academics. And everyone knows it, even though she never brags.

I smiled at my two best friends. "It *is* exciting," I told Fay.

"It's disastrous!" Cody wailed.

Fay and I stared blankly at Cody for a moment.

"What?" I questioned.

"*How?*" shrieked Fay.

"Well," Cody began, "*how* could a *math* test possibly be *exciting?*"

Again, Fay and I stared at Cody, until we burst out laughing, leaving Cody completely perplexed.

"What is it? Why are you guys laughing?" Cody asked.

"*Because,*" Fay snickered, "we were talking about the *wedding.* We weren't talking about math, you goose!"

Cody looked at us both, blinked, and then said, "Oh."

We continued on our walk, giggling here and there. However, when we saw a black pickup truck slowly drive near us, mud literally caked on its sides, we stopped, staring at it with suspicion.

"Who's *that?*" Fay hissed.

It wasn't very common for vehicles to drive around Wilsonville anyway, except when people went to church. No one ever drove quite *this* slowly, and it seemed as if this driver was watching us, whoever he was.

The truck drove off, and I hadn't been sure *whom* I had seen due to the figure's western-shaped hat blocking my view.

Snowflakes and Snickerdoodles

Chapter 6

"Do you really think that person was a stalker or something?" asked Cody.

"Who knows? Could be," Fay replied.

We were at Fay's house, planning to study for the upcoming math test.

Felicia's home was grand. It was an old, Victorian-style house, two stories in size, with white walls on the outside, gray shingles on the roof, a spacious porch, and stunning vines that climbed up and around the dwelling.

And to think, that was just the outside. The inside was just as beautiful, with crystal chandeliers, a spiraling staircase, pretty rugs, wooden bookcases, sofas, a fancy fireplace, and twin glass doors that led to the dining room.

"Since we don't know what that person was doing for sure, let's just be cautious and keep an eye out," I said.

Cody and Fay nodded.

"I agree," replied Fay.

"Yeah," Cody began, "for all we know, it could be another clue!"

Fay then picked up her math book. "We do need to review, though."

Cody groaned dramatically.

I laughed. "We'll survive, Cody."

Right now, we were in Fay's bedroom. Her room was painted pale pink, with a crystal chandelier on the ceiling. There was a dresser, a nightstand, and a bed, as well as some other things in her room. Her bedframe was white, and her bed had a partial canopy which was lacy and white. The bedspread was pink. On top of Felicia's white nightstand was a pink alarm clock, as well as a white lampstand that had a pink lampshade over it. Cody claimed there was too much pink in the room, but I thought it was just Fay's style.

"Besides," said Fay, "you told your parents you'd be back in time to help Ryker with the horses, which means we won't have to study super long anyway."

"Yeah, that's true," responded Cody, brightening a little.

Cody's brother, Ryker, didn't go to school in Wilsonville. There isn't a school here for his grade, so instead, he goes to Beaver City for school. Beaver City is about fifteen miles away.

Fay picked up her pencil, ready to start underlining things in her math book.

As she did so, Cody watched in misery and disappointment. She was underlining loads of things.

"When is the test anyway?" he asked. "I forgot."

"It's on Friday," Fay replied.

"In other words," I said, "we'd better start studying!"

* * *

We had done enough arithmetic study for the day, and Cody and I were about to leave Felicia's house.

We thanked Fay's mom, Mrs. Blackwood, for having us over. (Mr. Blackwood was still at work), Then we went to say goodbye to Leanne, Fay's little sister, who was only a year and three months old.

"Bye, Fay!" Cody and I said as we walked out the door.

Felicia waved. "Bye! See you tomorrow."

Kodiak and I then started walking down the sidewalk to our houses. The air was clean and crisp and cold. The sky was cloudy, but the clouds weren't as dark as they had been last Saturday.

"I wish it'd snow," Cody sighed as he longingly gazed up at the clouds.

"Me too," I replied.

Kodiak grinned. "Then me, you, and Fay could have a snowball fight!"

I laughed. "Definitely! Remember last year when we had that snowball fight, and Ryker literally built a fort?"

"Yes," Cody said with a happy snort. "It was us against him, but he still creamed us!"

"Well yeah," I replied and then grinned, "but Ryker had the fort."

"We'll get him this year!" chirped Cody, already plotting out his playful revenge.

"For sure!" I agreed.

During the next few minutes, we walked in silence, except for Cody humming cheerfully. There wasn't a person in sight except for the two of us.

"It's cold out here!" Cody exclaimed, straightening his gray, knit hat. (It had braided ties on each side and a fuzzy, red ball on the top.) His mom made it herself.

Laughing, I said, "It's so cold, your nose is pink!"

Cody instantly pulled his red- and gray-striped scarf over his nose.

"Are you serious?" he asked.

"Yes," I replied, smirking.

"This is *so* humiliating," Cody stated. He was eyeing his surroundings in hopes we wouldn't see anyone we knew.

"Your nose is the exact shade of Fay's bedroom walls," I teased.

"Not funny," retorted Cody, crossing his arms over his chest and huffing. Due to the cold air, his breath came out all foggy.

I snickered. "Don't worry, Code. Pink is a nice color."

"Not for my nose!"

"Your cheeks are pink too."

"*What?*"

When we saw one of the kids from school walking on the sidewalk across the road, Cody squeaked.

"Oh, *no!*" Cody yelped. "We've got to go another way!"

"Why?" I asked.

"*Because,*" hissed Cody, "Trevin is over there!"

I looked and saw that the strawberry-blond boy was right. Trevin was indeed the schoolboy on the other side of the street.

"Okay, we'll go another way," I replied.

Trevin Aragon was a bully, but by no means a stereotype. He was extremely smart, but he also was unfriendly and rude. He especially disliked Cody, as everyone was aware. Trevin was someone Cody and I really did *not* want to start a conversation with.

We turned a corner, deciding to take the long way to my house.

We were pretty quiet as we continued onward to my home. Cody constantly looked over his shoulder as if worried Trevin was following us, although I assumed that'd be unlikely.

"I don't think anyone's following us, Code."

"They could be!" responded Kodiak. Glancing over his shoulder again, he sighed in relief, mumbling quietly, "But… you're probably right."

It took a few minutes more, maybe five, until Cody was finally convinced no one was watching us.

"Guess you're right," said Cody with a tiny smile. "No one's here."

I smiled back and nodded. "Nothing to worry about."

Cody then started talking enthusiastically about how Nightfall was doing. He also was excited to start gardening again this spring, when the weather would be warm and cheerful. Likewise, Cody chatted about how he hoped to go fishing and be in rodeos.

I listened with interest, thinking about my own hopes and wishes for this year.

"That sounds fun," I chirped with a smile.

Cody grinned but then suddenly frowned, the gleeful look that was on his face just a moment earlier vanishing away.

"What is it?" I asked in worry, tensing up.

"*That*," Cody said hastily, pointing across the street. I followed his gaze and saw a tall man with a western-style hat. He was dressed in jeans, a western shirt, and boots.

"Why, that looks like the man we saw in the pickup truck yesterday!" I exclaimed in a whisper.

Cody nodded, his hazel eyes narrowing. "What do you suppose he's doing over there?"

I wasn't sure who the figure was. He had his back to us, and he was standing more in the shade, close to a wall of an abandoned and run-down building; it even had some broken windows. There was a fence, broken and torn down in some areas. He looked suspicious just standing there in the shade, occasionally looking from left to right.

Exchanging glances with me, Cody whispered, "Do you... Do you suppose, perhaps, this could lead to a clue?"

I shrugged and gave him a silent look that said, "Could be."

Pushing our backs up against the wall (in hopes it'd be harder for us—especially pink-nosed Cody— to be seen), we watched the man intently.

The man seemed to glance over his shoulder in both directions before pulling something out of his pocket. I couldn't see what it was, though, due to the fact he had his back to us.

Suddenly, the man shoved whatever he had been holding into his pocket and, turning to the left, swiftly walked off. In just a brief moment, he disappeared.

Cody slowly let out the big breath he had been holding. He turned and looked at me with wide eyes filled with astonishment.

"D-Did you see *that?*" Cody stammered, his face full of dread.

I gave him a blank look. "What do you mean?"

Cody pointed over to where the man had just been moments ago, then looked back at me, opened his mouth, closed it, and then finally choked out, "It was *him.*"

"Who?" I asked with concern, feeling a sinking feeling in my stomach.

"Maybe it's nothing…" said Cody, although the look on his face seemed to disagree.

"Who was it?" I inquired.

Cody hesitated for another moment. At last, he said: "Look, I know we don't have any proof about that guy doing anything suspicious, but…"

"But what?" I asked.

Cody sighed. "It was Uriah Harper."

* * *

"It was probably nothing," Cody said, kicking a rock off the sidewalk and onto the road.

After seeing Uriah at that run-down building yesterday, I had called Fay and told her all about it. Now, Kodiak, Felicia, and I were walking to school.

Nodding, Felicia said, "We really don't have *proof* about Mr. Harper doing, or planning, anything wrong. However, we do know to keep an eye on him."

"It was a little suspicious," I agreed.

Fay sighed. "We don't know anything for *sure,* it seems. For all we know, if there was a criminal from three years ago, they could be *miles* away; they could be living in *Hawaii!*"

Cody suddenly beamed despite the unease. "Pineapples!"

I had to laugh out loud at that. "You've got a point, Fay. But, at least we do have *some* clues, right?"

Nodding in agreement with my statement, Cody chirped, "Yeah! And besides, there might be another clue just around the corner—literally."

That got Fay to brighten some. "True," she replied with a small smile.

My friends and I then grew quiet, thinking to ourselves silently as we walked. Cody, however, was nearly skipping in his cowboy boots.

Feeling a chilly wind, I looked up at the gray clouds that covered the sky. *Maybe we will get some snow after all.*

I quickly pushed those thoughts aside, though, when Cody abruptly stopped, making Fay bump into him and then me bump into Fay. We couldn't regain our balance, and we all fell in one big heap.

"Whoa!" I exclaimed.

"Ow!" Fay yelped.

"I got it!" Cody shouted.

Fay and I looked at him, perplexed.

"You got what?" asked Fay.

"An idea!" cheered Cody.

"An idea?" I inquired. "For what?"

Cody grinned, sitting up. "For finding clues!"

"What kind of idea?" Fay questioned, groaning a little as she turned over on her back and then sat up.

Still sitting on the ground, Cody grinned even more widely. "So, you know how we were just talking about Uriah?" he asked.

I nodded, rising to my feet. "Yeah. What about him?"

"Well," Cody began, "suppose we go see Miss Caden and try to see if she knows anything."

"Why, Cody," exclaimed Fay, "that's a wonderful idea!"

"I agree," I said. "Maybe we could ask her after school today or tomorrow."

"Yeah! But… what do we say?" asked Cody.

Fay rose up off the ground, picking up her backpack. "That's a good question. I'm not quite sure."

"Perhaps we can just try to think of something when we get there?" I asked, a little uncertain.

Cody shrugged and stood up. "I guess so. It's worth a try, right?"

Nodding, Fay said, "Yeah! It's better than nothing."

Suddenly, Cody started digging around in his cowboy boot.

"Cody," I began in a confused voice, "what *are* you doing?"

Cody was silent for a moment, continuing to search his boot. Fay and I watched him with raised eyebrows.

"Oh, here is it!" Cody exclaimed happily as he pulled out a few dollar bills.

Fay stared at the cash in his hand for a moment before saying, "Why is there money in your boot?"

Cody shoved the money back into his footwear and grinned. "Big bucks, aren't they? Mom wanted me to make a quick trip to the store after school. Just wanted to make sure the cash was still safe and sound."

I laughed a little at that. Only Cody would walk around with money in his shoe.

"Kodiak," began Fay, "you're very... uh... unique."

Cody gave us an enormous grin with his eyes closed and said in a pleased manner, "I know."

* * *

The bell rang at school, signaling that my friends and I had "endured" our sixth-grade day, as Cody had put it.

"So... much... math homework..." whimpered Cody.

"It's about as much as we always have," replied Fay with a smirk.

"My point still stands."

I laughed at Cody's statement and began walking down the street with my friends. We were going to talk to Miss Caden about Uriah the next day. Fay and I decided to join Cody on the shopping errand he had, courtesy of his mother. The store was on the way to my house anyway.

It didn't take long until we were at the entrance of the store and, with Cody pushing open the door, all of us filed in.

A small bell sounded overhead, signaling our arrival.

The store, to be exact, was a general store. The walls and floors are made of wood, and so are the shelves. There were boxes and barrels filled with various things. The building itself looks rather old. It was a simple place, and quiet too.

"So, Cody," I began, "what *did* your mom need you to pick up?"

"I guess she needs cinnamon; we're all out," responded Cody, casually.

"Cinnamon?" asked Felicia. "What's she making?"

Cody beamed. "Snickerdoodles!"

"Oh, that sounds delicious!" I said.

"Yeah," agreed Kodiak, "especially if you dip them in milk."

"For sure!" chirped Fay.

Snickerdoodles have always been a favorite among my friends and me. Whenever we went on a picnic, snickerdoodles were there. For the first day of summer vacation, we had snickerdoodles. For the *last* day of summer vacation, we had snickerdoodles. It was kind of a thing. Cody even made a song about the cinnamon-flavored cookies. They were just that *good*.

We trooped in a line over to where we could find some cinnamon, the floorboards creaking beneath our feet.

"There it is," said Fay, pointing over to a shelf with various spices and things.

"Sweet!" Cody replied, grabbing a container of cinnamon off the shelf.

"Well, if you're looking for something sweet, try this," I said, pointing to a tub of sugar.

Cody snorted and playfully rolled his eyes at my lame pun.

Fay laughed aloud. "Good one, Lia."

A few moments later, Cody was paying the cashier, chatting happily as he did so. I was looking around the store from where I was standing, and I saw Doctor Layton across the building looking at some tools. I noticed him holding a tool that looked like a pair of pliers or something like that. However, one side of the top part was sharp and pointy. He was also holding a crowbar.

"Look, Fay," I said, tilting my head to where Doctor Layton was.

Fay looked at the doctor, and then she looked at me. "What is it?"

"Look at what he's holding," I replied in a whisper. "Doesn't it look kind of suspicious?"

For a moment, Fay looked at the tools Mr. Layton was holding.

"Not really…" said Fay.

"Well, he's a doctor, so why is he holding those kinds of things?" I asked quietly.

"That's true. I guess you're right," Fay replied.

Cody was unaware of our conversation. "Ready to head out?" he asked.

"I guess in a second," I responded.

"Cody, what's the plier-like thing with the sharp edge in Doctor Layton's hand?" Fay asked quietly so the doctor wouldn't hear her.

"That?" asked Cody. "That's a pair of fencing pliers."

"Why's he buying that?" I inquired.

Cody shrugged. "I don't know."

"Maybe he's just… fixing something?" asked Felicia, slightly uncertain.

"Maybe…" I said. "Or perhaps it's another clue…"

Cody and Fay's eyebrows shot up.

"Oh, come on, Lia," said Cody. "Surely you wouldn't think something like *that*."

"Why not?" I questioned.

Kodiak was about to say something, but Fay cleared her throat.

"It's worth at least contemplating," she stated.

Cody was silent for a moment. "I suppose that's true..."

I nodded. "It can't hurt to consider it, anyway."

Fay looked rather thoughtful and was quiet. "I do wonder..." she mumbled under her breath.

"You wonder what?" Cody asked, tilting his head to the side a little.

"I was just thinking about all the possible clues we've collected so far. I'm still trying to make sense of it all," Fay admitted.

"I am, too," I replied.

Cody nodded a little, and then he said quietly, "I think we're still doing good, though—great even. After all, *some* possible clues are better than *no* possible clues..."

Fay smiled a little, apparently feeling somewhat relieved. "That's true."

"I agree," I told both of my friends as we began heading out of the store.

The moment we left, we instantly stopped in our tracks.

Delicate and small *snowflakes* were falling from the cloud-covered sky.

"Snow!" Cody yelled in shocked delight.

I beamed and all, but Fay literally *rejoiced* in laughter!

The flakes were small, but they were falling quite well. I wasn't sure if they'd stick or not, but at least we had something.

"Maybe we'll even get to have a snowball fight!" Cody cheered while trying to catch the falling snow on his tongue.

"That'd be great!" I replied.

"It would!" Fay said with a grin. "We need to beat Ryker, anyway."

Cody nodded. "Yes! He's really going to have it coming to him this time if the snow sticks!"

I snickered. "Oh yes, he certainly will!"

The three of us began walking down the sidewalk, talking about various snow-themed things we could do assuming the snow wouldn't melt before we got the chance.

I beamed, pushing my worries aside for now. They could wait, at least for a little while. Looking at the softly falling snow, I began to feel better about the whole search for clues.

THE PURSUIT OF EVIDENCE

Chapter 7

The next day, my friends and I had finished school. We were going to ask Miss Caden about Uriah now, as a matter of fact.

As Cody, Fay, and I walked over to her desk (trying to stay calm and casual and normal), we honestly weren't quite sure how to begin the conversation.

Miss Caden looked up from where she was tidying things on her desk. "Hello, children."

"Hello," we said back, a little awkwardly.

Fay decided to give it her best shot.

"So, Miss Caden," she began, "how are things going between you and Uriah?"

If Cody had been drinking anything, chances were he would have just spit it out, as he made some sound between a strangled cough and a snort at Fay's statement.

Miss Caden, Fay, and I all stared at Cody for a moment due to the sound of his strange noise, so that he ended up somewhat blushing in embarrassment.

Clearing his throat and acting slightly sheepish, Cody said, "Sorry, continue."

Miss Caden smiled. "It's all right, Kodiak. And it's been generally quite well, Felicia."

Well, it was good to hear that things were *generally* well, of course, but I really wanted to dig deeper. Obviously, we couldn't just expect Miss Caden to spill out anything and everything.

Suddenly, Cody blurted out, "Miss Caden, what *do* you mean by 'generally quite well'?"

"Well, things have been busy, for one," responded our teacher.

I felt like my heart sighed inside. Was that really all? Were things just busy? But no, we had seen Uriah doing *something*. What was it? We had to find out!

I decided on taking a possibly crazy chance. I abruptly burst out, "Miss Caden, we saw Uriah over by an abandoned building. Do you know anything about why he was there?"

Cody and Fay both gave me a confused face that seemed to say, "What *are* you doing?" I just gave them a "Trust me," look in return.

"An abandoned building?" asked Miss Caden. "How curious."

I nodded. "Yeah! Do you know anything about it?"

"I'm not fully sure," said my teacher. "However, Uriah has been more…"

Miss Caden was quiet for a long moment as if choosing her next words carefully.

"More what?" Cody asked.

"Well, more spaced out or so—like he's deep in thought. And he's been out at places I've never been to," Miss Caden replied almost as if she was just thinking to herself.

"Oh…" murmured Felicia. I could tell she was thinking about how this could be a probable clue.

Miss Caden then smiled. "But I wouldn't worry about it, children. I'm sure all's well," she said in assurance and faith.

I let out a breath I hadn't known I had been holding. My teacher could really make things feel less stressful!

"Miss Caden," Cody said softly and a little unexpectedly, "what's that?"

Cody was pointing to a silver, heart-shaped pendant—it wasn't on a chain, however.

"It's a locket, Kodiak," said Miss Caden with a gentle smile. "It was a gift my grandfather gave me a few years ago. I received it after I moved here to teach and help him at his house."

Gazing at the necklace piece, Fay said, "It's very beautiful."

"Thank you, Felicia."

Cody quietly said, with a sympathizing tone in his voice, "And I think he'd be happy to see you still teaching and living here in Wilsonville."

"I agree," I declared.

"Yes, I think so too," said Miss Caden. "It's been four years now…"

We were all silent for a moment, until Miss Caden told us, "You'd best hurry along now, children. It won't do to have you missing out on your lunch, will it?"

"No, it really won't," replied Cody, gazing wistfully (and hungrily) out into the hallway, past the classroom door.

"Thank you for your time, Miss Caden," Fay said.

"Oh, of course, darlings," our teacher replied, smiling. "Anytime."

* * *

"It's got to count for something, right?" asked Cody later that afternoon, taking a bite out of a snickerdoodle his mom made.

I was at Cody's house with Fay. We were going to study some more for the math test, but now we were talking about our clues, especially the possible clues we found out while talking to Miss Caden earlier.

"I think so," said Fay as she turned through the pages of the math book.

Cody frowned a little. I knew it was because Fay was turning through the arithmetic book, which meant we were about to study.

I laughed. "Come on, Cody, studying's not so bad."

"It is when you're a dunce at math."

Fay looked up from her textbook upon hearing Cody's statement. "Well, I wouldn't say you are a *dunce.*"

"Trevin would. And so would *way* over half the kids at school," Cody replied.

"Yeah, but Trevin thinks everyone's a dunce if they aren't quite as smart as him," I responded.

Cody smirked a little. "That *is* true, to an extent."

"Besides," chirped Fay, "you're obviously the best in art class."

Cody shrugged modestly. "If you say so."

"I do say so," Fay firmly responded.

I nodded in agreement. "You *are* the best at art, Code!"

Cody grinned some and laughed in a slightly nervous, slightly modest fashion. "Well, maybe I can also become the best in math, too, if I study enough."

I grinned back. "Sure you can."

Out of the blue, a very familiar voice said, "Hey, Cross Eyes, girls."

"Hi and hello, Pitchfork," replied Cody, causally biting into his beloved snickerdoodle.

Sure enough, Cody's older brother had come into the bedroom, which was where we were talking and getting ready to study.

Ryker smirked. "'Hi' *and* 'hello'? You just double-greeted me."

"I know," Cody responded almost haughtily, smirking back.

"Oh, hey, Rhys!" Fay and I greeted with waves as we smiled warmly.

Rhys was, of course, Ryker's nickname.

"So, what are you guys doing up here?" Ryker asked. "Attempting mathematics?"

"Well, we're about to, anyway," said Cody.

Ryker nodded. "Good luck, guys. I got a truckload of my own homework, actually, but if you want some help, you know where to find me."

"We do?" Fay asked.

"Yeah," said Ryker, "in the kitchen, where all the snickerdoodles are. Catch ya later, guys."

It was at that moment Ryker darted out of Cody's room and started running down the stairs. Of course, Cody jumped up from where he was sitting and sprinted out of the room after his older brother, shrieking, "Don't you dare!" in attempt to keep Ryker from taking *all* of his precious cookies.

As we heard the two brothers dashing into the kitchen, Fay and I exchanged glances.

"Wow…" I murmured, a smirk tugging at my lips, "that was fast."

Fay nodded and smirked as well. "It was indeed. Shall we study while we wait for them to settle matters?"

I laughed. "Sure, why not?"

* * *

About an hour and a half later, I was walking to my house with Fay. The "cookie duel" had gone fine. No pots were broken and no plants were knocked over in Ryker and Cody's attempts to keep each other away from the delicious treats. In fact, they had even given Fay and me one each. The cookies were wonderful, as Mrs. Nobleman's desserts always are.

We had even gotten some riding in after studying.

Anyway, Fay and I were walking down the sidewalk as we chatted happily. Fay was telling me all about this lovely, yellow dress with a blue jacket she had seen when she was out of town for an afternoon recently. It was good to get my mind off the mysteries my friends and I had been trying to discover.

"So, after seeing it, it gave me a splendid idea," said Fay, beaming.

"Oh?" I asked. "And what might that be?"

"Well, I remembered the yellow fabric I had received for my birthday last year. I had been saving it. I suppose I could sew a yellow dress very much like the one I had seen at the shop. And I already have a blue jacket quite close to the one I saw," explained Felicia.

I nodded. "That's a wonderful idea!"

Fay has always been talented at sewing. (I was literally wearing a flannel shirt she made me as we walked down the sidewalk.) To be honest, crochet is more of my thing. What's strange, however, is that Fay and I *cannot* knit by *any* means; but what makes it *really* strange is that Cody actually can! We tease him about it, and he always worries that word of his knitting abilities will go around until Trevin finds out. What makes it even more amusing is that *Ryker* was the one who taught him how to knit. Of course, Cody prefers painting *much* more.

But, anyway, another thing about Fay is that she *loves* pretty dresses. Don't get the wrong idea, however, because even though her family is wealthy, Felicia is *frugal*, or in other words, wise with her money. She can always make a pretty dress at a low cost, which I find commendable. It isn't just that, though. Fay likes things to be tidy and clean. Cody and I found that out when we saw her wardrobe was literally organized by color. Cody always teases her about that.

"It was a lovely dress I saw," said Felicia as we continued to my house. "It wasn't overly frilly— although I do love frilly things—but still pretty, so that it was good for multiple kinds of occasions."

I smiled. "Always thinking things through, Fay. And that's a good thing—smart, too—even if you do organize your closet by color."

Fay laughed. "Thanks, Lia. If you want, I can organize your closet for you, too."

"I think I'm good!" I said, snickering. "Besides, Cody would think I betrayed him if my wardrobe were organized by color."

"True," responded Fay. "I really don't know how he finds anything in that closet of his, though. It's a dreadful mess."

"Well, he is Cody. He has his ways, you know," I told my friend.

"Yeah, that's right. Oh! I forgot to mention, Lia," chirped Fay, "I asked Mother yesterday evening if you could come over tonight for a sleepover—if you can and would like to."

"I'd love to, Fay. I'll ask Grandmother when I get home. Do you want to come into the house for a minute?" I inquired, seeing that we were getting close to my home now.

"Sure," said Fay. "This will be fun!"

I nodded in agreement. "Yeah, it will be!"

Fay and I slowed down our pace, though, when we heard a truck coming around.

"Oh, *look*," Fay whispered, tilting her head over toward the vehicle.

Instantly recognizing who was driving the truck, I gasped softly.

"Why, that's Uriah!" I exclaimed in a rather large whisper.

"Come on, let's continue walking to your house," said Fay. "It'll make us seem like we don't suspect him."

So Felicia and I both continued walking, but we each quietly eyed Uriah in his truck, our faces filled with distrust.

Uriah's vehicle was the same one Cody, Fay, and I had seen the day we found out about Miss Caden's engagement. The black pickup truck drove by very slowly, as it had on that day.

"He seems to be following us," Fay mumbled to me. "It's like he's watching to see where we're going or what we're doing…"

I gave a tiny nod. "You're right. I don't like it at all…"

"Agreed…" Felicia replied. "It's creepy."

"Oh, let's just go inside the house!" I whispered. "Before he gets any closer."

"Well we can't just run," hissed Fay. "We have to act normal."

"You're right," I murmured. "But it can't hurt to pick up the pace just slightly more."

Fay gave a small nod. "That's true. Let's try that."

And so, Fay and I started walking down the sidewalk a little more swiftly.

"I say! It's like he's only going a mile an hour!" exclaimed Fay, quietly as she could.

"Maybe he is…" I muttered.

At last, after what seemed to have been much longer than it really was, the charcoal-colored pickup drove off.

"Oh, *phew!*" gasped Felicia. "It felt like he'd never leave."

"*Now* can we make a run for it?" I questioned.

Fay let out a small laugh. "You sound like Cody. But oh, yes!"

We blitzed like bullets to my house. When we reached my home, we threw open the door, ran in, and then slammed it. As I locked the door, we panted like wild hyenas.

Fay put a hand over her heart. My own heart was rapidly beating from our sprint to the house.

"Where is your grandmother?" asked Fay.

"I don't know—probably in her room. Let's go check."

A few moments later, we reached Grandmother's room and saw she was indeed there.

Grandmother looked up from where she was writing down some things on a paper—a shopping list, I think. "Why, Lydia! I was just about to go see what the noise was all about. Hello, Felicia, it's so good to see you today."

"Hi!" Fay greeted with a smile. "How are you?"

"I'm well today. Are you girls all right, though? I could hear the clatter when you both ran into the house. Do I need to grab the shotgun?"

"Oh, no, no, Grandmother—that's all right!" I said quickly.

Grandmother always kept her shotgun in her room, in case she needed it.

She nodded. "Well, I'm relieved to hear it, then."

Suddenly, I remembered why Fay was here with me in the first place. "Oh, I almost forgot!" I burst out. "Fay asked me if I could come over to her house for a sleepover tonight."

"I already checked with Mother," added Fay.

"May I go?" I asked.

"Of course you can go," Grandmother replied with a smile.

"Thank you!" Fay and I both blurted out at the same time.

Grandmother smiled. "Have fun, loves. Now, go get packed!"

Fay and I laughed.

Saluting, I shouted, "Yes, Ma'am!"

Paths of the Woods

Chapter 8

"What do you suppose Uriah was up to?" Fay asked me.

I was at Fay's house, sitting cross-legged on the floor. Fay was sitting on her bed behind me, French-braiding my hair.

"Oh, I don't know," I replied. "Could be anything."

That moment, the phone rang.

Fay was about to get up and grab it, but then the phone stopped ringing, and we could hear Mrs. Blackwood say, "Hello?"

"I wonder who's calling," I said.

"Perhaps it's one of Father's friends from work," responded Fay.

As it turned out, we didn't have to wait more than a minute to find out who was calling, because Mrs. Blackwood called out, "Felicia, it's for you!"

"Be right back. Hold this?" Fay asked, wanting me to hold my halfway finished braid before it came undone.

"Sure," I replied with a smile.

Fay got up and left. I waited patiently for her return, feeling quite curious.

A few minutes passed by, leaving me with my own suspense-filled thoughts.

I had gone through every possible person I could think of that might be calling, and why they would be, when Fay came back with a facial expression I couldn't quite place.

"Who was it?" I asked.

"Cody," replied Fay. "Apparently, he was walking home after picking up a book in the bus, and he heard some people talking by that abandoned building you told me about."

"Oh!" I exclaimed. "Who were they?"

"Well, he looked around the corner, and low and behold, it was Uriah! But he couldn't make out whom he was talking to, because it was already getting dark."

I nodded. "Anything else?"

"Yeah, he unintentionally overheard them talking about meeting at that abandoned building around midnight."

"Around midnight…?" I asked. "That sounds suspicious."

"That's what Cody and I thought too. Also, Cody had a run-in with Trevin on his way to the bus."

"Oh, that doesn't sound good," I said. "What happened?"

"I'm not fully sure; he didn't go into detail," said Fay as she sat down on her bed and started to braid my hair again.

I nodded a little. "Well, hopefully it wasn't too bad or anything."

"Yeah, I hope it wasn't," said Fay.

We were then silent for a moment, just thinking.

I wonder what Uriah's planning…

* * *

I had tried my best to sleep that night but to no avail. Eventually, I found myself just staring up at the ceiling.

It must be past eleven at night now.

Sighing, I turned to my side and looked over at Felicia.

"Fay, are you awake?" I hissed.

Fay sat up in her bed. "Well, now I am."

"Oh, I just *can't* sleep," I said. "I keep thinking about how Uriah's going to that abandoned building."

"I've thought of that as well," responded Fay in a whisper. "What do you suppose we do? What if he's going to do *something* tonight?"

"Well," I said softly, "then we'll have to stop him."

Fay stared at me for a moment like I had lost it.

"B-B-But," she stuttered, "it could be dangerous!"

"Yes, but if he isn't guilty, then we'll be fine over there. And if he *is* about to commit a crime or something... we can't let him succeed!"

Fay hesitated for a moment but then finally said quietly, "You're right."

* * *

So that was how I found myself, just minutes later, carefully tiptoeing down the stairs with Fay in the dead of night, both of us now in our normal attire rather than our pajamas, of course.

We both slipped on our coats, winter hats, and scarves, quietly as we could, knowing the winter weather of mid-February was bound to be cold, as it had been all this season.

Silent as a mouse, I opened the front door, Fay and I sneaking out of the house and into the night.

The air outside was indeed chilly, and I shivered at once when I felt the cold and crisp breeze rush past me. The sky was clear, the stars hung high overhead, and the moon was just a sliver, rather than a full moon, so that it proved to be significantly dark out. However, the coating of snow upon the ground looked bright in the moonlight.

The whole town seemed asleep.

"Oh, wait—let me grab something," said Fay.

I was expecting her to carefully open the door and then soundlessly go into her house, but instead, she stayed where she was, on the front porch. I was even more shocked when she began to dig around in her boot.

I just stared at her blankly for a moment.

Finally, Fay pulled out a flashlight.

"Here we are!" she chirped with a smirk. "Now we can at least see. Cody had a good idea with the whole boot thing."

I blinked as I looked at the flashlight but then let out a tiny laugh. "Good idea, Fay."

"Thank you. We probably shouldn't use the flashlight that much, though, since we don't want to draw attention to ourselves and all."

I nodded. "Sharp as a tack as always, Fay."

Felicia giggled a little, "Thanks."

We quickly turned solemn again, however, as we remembered the task at hand.

"Where *is* the building, Lia?" whispered Felicia softly. "You and Cody never did tell me."

It suddenly dawned on me that Fay was right. "I'm so sorry! I totally forgot."

Fay gave a nod, putting a finger to her lips, as she looked over her shoulder and at her house. "It's all right."

"Here," I said, tilting my head toward the pasture behind her house. "I'll show you the way."

Stealthily as we could, we snuck over to the Fay's family's pasture. As we kept walking, we neared a mass of trees, some small woods. Fay's father planted most of the trees when he moved to this house years ago. My friends and I always like to play in the grove, but now, at this late hour, it was much spookier and much less enjoyable. My fingers felt numb with cold due to the especially chilly night. I shoved my hands into the pockets of my violet-colored, woolen coat.

We hurried into the woods and then tried to make our way through the trees as fast as we could. However, Fay and I had to be careful; even though we were on a path, more than once we started to trip.

"If Cody were here," said Fay, shivering some from the cold, "he'd have already fallen flat on his face."

I smiled a little, despite the unease. "Yeah, he would have."

As we continued to make our way through the woods, it soon got thicker with trees.

"*Oh,* it is *so* very creepy out here tonight," moaned Fay.

I just nodded, concentrating on not losing my footing due to the fallen twigs and occasional branches. Thankfully, the path Fay and I were on was shoveled, so we didn't have to walk in the snow. I ducked under some branches and looked down at my feet, trying to avoid the boughs that stuck out from the trees.

I wasn't even fully sure what part of the woods Fay and I were in.

"We must be about halfway through the woods now since the beginning of the woods is thinner, then it gets thicker in the middle, and then it starts to fade out toward the end," said Fay a little to herself.

I nodded. "Doesn't this path lead to your tree house?" There were a few different small paths around the woods.

"Yeah, that's right," said Fay.

We continued through the woods mostly in silence, dodging some of the tree limbs that were very long and stuck out in front of us.

My toes were cold now. I was just glad to be at least wearing my tall boots rather than my ankle boots—not to mention that I was extremely thankful I had decided to bring my knit hat when I came over for the sleepover at Fay's house.

The two of us then saw Felicia's tree house, which has always reminded me of an enchanted cottage. Fay's father had made it himself, and it was very impressive looking.

However, instead of the tree house looking enchanted, I felt it looked haunted that night.

At once, I heard someone breath sharply.

I looked at Fay, a little perplexed.

"It wasn't I," she said.

Fay turned on the flashlight. She shined it at the tree house and then all around us.

"We're getting close to the edge of the woods," she said in a whisper.

I nodded, narrowing my eyes as I looked around the woods.

Then I heard someone break into a run.

Only for a second did I exchange shocked glances with Fay before she and I darted off after the person. Whoever this person was, he or she seemed to be coming from ahead of us.

My breath came out like smoke due to the cold, and my feet pounded on the path that led out of the woods. I didn't dare trip.

That's when I saw *him,* a shadowy figure in the light of the crescent moon. He was running—running through the woods. I wondered how he didn't slip on the snow.

Fay and I didn't hesitate for a minute. We sprinted after him at once.

It didn't take long until we caught up with him. I managed to run just fast enough to get in front of him, and then he had to stop.

Of course, he instantly tried to turn around and run the other way, but Felicia was behind him.

A tall, somewhat thin boy with dark-brown hair scowled at us in the slightly moonlit woods.

I gasped softly when I recognized him.

The boy narrowed his eyes. "What do *you* want?"

Felicia's eyebrows shot up. "Trevin?"

The boy was, indeed, Trevin Aragon.

Rolling his eyes, Trevin said in annoyance, "*Yes.* What are you bothering me for?"

"What are you doing out here?" I inquired.

"I could ask you the same thing," Trevin retorted with a scoff.

Turning to Fay, I gave her a look that said, "He does have a point."

Trevin turned on his heel, about to leave. "Look, stop trying to get involved in other people's lives and business. It's *rude.*"

Fay took a step forward.

"*Excuse* me?" she said, crossing her arms over her chest. "For your info, *you've* been *trespassing* on my father's property. Because of this, it technically *is* my business."

If Cody were here, I was sure he would have said, "Good one, Fay!"

Trevin, stunned by Felicia's response, held his tongue.

"Besides," I began quietly, "maybe we could help you…"

Fay turned to me with a curious expression. Trevin, however, narrowed his eyes and snorted rudely.

"I don't need any help from *a couple of giggling schoolgirls,*" he scoffed.

It was at this moment that Trevin sharply turned on his heel, as he had a moment before, and ran off before Fay and I could say anything else.

Fay sighed and turned toward me. I put a rather cold hand on her shoulder, saying, "Let's just leave him to himself. It's clear he doesn't want our help, and besides: We've got to get to the abandoned building."

Fay nodded. "You're right. It's already been a while now..."

So, we broke off into a run at once down the path; in a moment, there were just a few trees in sight, and then, Fay and I were out of the woods.

"All right," I said, "now I think if we just take a left..."

There was no time to waste. I hardly noticed how cold I was. I was just thinking about the building. My mind went in circles as I tried to guess how long it might take us to get there. I wasn't even sure what time it was.

What if it's already midnight?

But then I recognized Dearborn Street, and I sighed in relief. The building wasn't *too* far from Dearborn Street.

"Now where?" asked Fay in a whisper.

I slowed down and looked at the dimly lit town.

"We take a left," I said at last.

Silently hurrying along the dirt roads, the snow crunching beneath our feet, Fay and I made our way through Wilsonville.

I have lived in Wilsonville my whole life, and I know my way around. Despite the fact it was dark outside, I still felt confident I was walking the right way.

As Fay and I quietly snuck around the town, I noticed the general store. That instantly brought my mind to just days before, when Cody, Fay, and I were looking for cinnamon. That's when I realized someone was missing—Cody. Fay and I were possibly about to uncover the whole mystery, and Cody wasn't even with us. I immediately felt sad, and a little guilty. However, I knew it couldn't be helped—not now, anyway.

"Lia?"

I snapped out of my thoughts.

"Sorry, what, Fay?"

Fay smiled a little. "You looked deep in thought. What's on your mind?"

"Oh," I said a little sheepishly, "I was just thinking about how here we are, maybe going to finally find out what happened three years ago, but Cody's not even here with us."

Fay nodded. "Yeah, I've been thinking about that too…"

"If we do finally find out… what do you think Cody will think?"

Fay, after some thought, replied: "What do I think Cody will think? I think we'd better not think about what Cody will think; that's what I think."

Once processing what Fay was *thinking,* I gave one nod. "You're right."

And then I stared at the run-down and abandoned building now in front of me.

"We're here."

Broken Glass

Chapter 9

I shuddered as I looked at the large structure in front of me. The building looked creepy and mysterious in the dim light of the crescent moon.

Taking a deep breath, I silently began to make my way over to the building. Fay followed behind me.

"Lia," she began in a soft whisper, "are you sure this is a good idea?"

I felt dreadfully nervous and wondered if my choice would lead to a grave folly, but I steadied my shaking hands and replied as determinedly, but quietly, as I could.

"I don't know, Fay, but I cannot make the mistake of going back now. Not when I've come so far. This is our chance! We could be about to stop something awful from happening, and as far as I'm concerned, that's what matters right now."

Fay was quiet for a moment. She then said a little nervously, but also in agreement, "Well… then let's go."

Quieter than a cat stalking its prey, we snuck to the right side of the building, and I held my breath as I felt the snow crunch beneath my feet.

There were two windows on this side of the building. Fay and I went toward the window closer to the back. Then, crouching some, we peered through the cracked glass.

From what I could see through the window, the room inside was large and mostly bare. The floor had no carpet; it was concrete. The walls were chipping paint, and gray. I noticed an empty shelf on the wall, a little crooked to its left. There was a chain dangling from the wall, connected to a lightbulb. Honestly, I hoped no one lived there; the homely room didn't seem like much of a living place…

Fay exchanged glances with me. "It's repulsive…" she murmured.

I gave a tiny nod and then turned back to look through the window.

There was, of course, a door in the room. It was ajar

I squinted to see past the door, but I couldn't see much—just a wooden floor and the same old, gray walls. Nothing was interesting. Where was Uriah, anyway?

As if on cue, I saw the door get pushed open. I instantly ducked down, worried I'd get caught. Fay did the same.

I could hear, faintly hear, footsteps behind the door's entrance, and I shuddered at the thought of Uriah.

Fay gave me a look of shocked fear, and I felt that my own facial expression looked the same.

Then I heard more footsteps. I held my breath.

Suddenly, an *unfamiliar* voice said, "I don't know how much time we have."

I was instantly curious, so I slowly peeked into the room.

Uriah was leaning against a wall, legs crossed, cowboy hat pulled low, looking totally relaxed. Someone else was there as well.

Uriah said, "Then we'll have to do it tonight."

At Uriah's words, my eyes went wide with shock, and Fay sucked in her breath.

The other person replied, "You're right."

He then turned around toward the window Fay and I were by.

I quickly ducked and pushed away from the window. Fay did the same, but on the other side, farther away from me.

Then the curtains were roughly shut.

Felicia turned to me with a look that said, "Now what?"

I looked up at the window and then looked at Fay before mouthing, "Let's go behind the building."

So, we rose up and began to make our way over to the back silently.

There were three windows on this side. Two were a normal size, but the one in the middle was huge. One window allowed us to see into the room where Uriah was. Thankfully, the windows on this side of the building didn't have any curtains.

I peeked through the window, carefully remaining as conspicuous as possible.

Then I heard Uriah say, "Let's go. There isn't time to lose."

The other man nodded. "Yes. Now is the time."

The two then walked out of the room, Uriah quietly shutting the door behind him.

I turned to Fay, worried.

"Lia, we have to follow them…" Fay said softly.

I nodded. "Yes, we do."

* * *

It seemed to be a long time as Fay and I waited for Uriah and the other person to leave the building. However, it had only been several minutes, most likely. Fay and I had been hiding close to the front of the building, both of us pushed closely against the wall. I felt very tired, and the numb, bitter cold seemed to vibrate through my very bones.

Once the door had opened, though, I forgot about the chilliness.

I watched as the two suspicious characters locked the building's door. I observed them walking at a fast pace to the sidewalk.

When they were a little way away, but still able to be seen, Fay and I slowly rose to our feet.

The two of us then slipped into the shadows and began to trail after Uriah and his comrade, making our way through the snow as quietly as we could.

As we snuck around, I wondered what Uriah and the other person (whoever he was) were up to. Both Fay and I were lost in our own thoughts. The whole night felt perpetual.

I then noticed, through the streetlights of the town, soft white flurries falling from the sky. It was snowing.

Cody will be happy tomorrow when he sees the snow, I thought. If only he knew what Fay and I had been up to!

"Oh, Lia," Fay said to me in a whisper, "look where Uriah and that stranger are going."

I quickly noticed what part of Wilsonville we were at.

Turning to Fay with dread, I whispered back, "This is the way to the school!"

Felicia nodded. "I wonder what they're up to…"

"We're about to find out," I replied quietly.

* * *

Just a few moments later, I found myself at the edge of the school. There was a nervous feeling in the pit of my stomach, and I was very worried.

The school was robbed before… What if that is going to happen again?

I narrowed my eyes at Uriah and his comrade. *What are they up to?*

I was jerked out of my thoughts, however, when Fay gasped and put a hand to her mouth.

Fay pointed a slightly shaking hand over to the school, and I saw what had her afraid. Uriah and the other person were sneaking around the school building!

Turning to me with an uneasy expression, Fay whispered, "I-I think they're going to break in."

Distressed, I nodded. "Oh, Fay, we've got to do something!"

"But what?" asked Felicia.

By this point, I wasn't *just* afraid. I was also curious!

"Let's look through the windows," I said. "Maybe we'll find something out that way."

"All right," Fay agreed. "And it's safer than going inside the school…"

I gave a small nod, and then we waited for Uriah and his comrade to go into the school building.

Once the two suspicious characters quietly snuck inside, I carefully went over to one of the school's windows. Fay followed.

Peeking in, I quickly scanned the inside of the building. It was hard to see, however, since it was so dark inside.

"I don't really see anything," I told Fay in a whisper.

Fay then peeked in as well. Sighing, she said, "You're right. It's too dark…"

"Now what do we do?" I asked, feeling frustrated that our plan wasn't working.

Fay thought for a moment. "We could tell someone—an adult—you know."

I considered that. "Yeah, but what if we are too late by then?"

"That's true," Fay said. "But we're only twelve. How can we stop a crime?"

"I don't know…" I replied, feeling a little lost. I gazed through one of the windows again, only half paying attention. However, something caught my eye.

What?

I squinted.

"Lia?" I heard Fay ask. "What is it?"

"Just a second, Fay," I mumbled.

What's going on in there?

The door that led out of the classroom and into the hallway was slightly opened. I was sure I just saw something fall. Suddenly, I saw the classroom door open, and I ducked.

"Oh, we've *got* to go get some help!" I whispered.

"What's happened?" asked Fay. "What is it?"

"I think Uriah and the other person are going to rob the school. We can't stop a robbery, but—"

I was cut off short when, about ten feet away, a window shattered.

Crushed glass went all over the snowy ground, and I instantly threw my arms over my face in an attempt to keep from getting cut. Then another window broke, only this time closer.

I suddenly realized that there was a good chance the window Fay and I were by might be broken next.

I bolted up from where I was and darted over to a wall near the school building's entrance.

Fay was next to me in an instant, looking as white as a ghost.

Feeling very shaky, I asked worriedly, "You aren't cut, are you?"

Fay shook her head once. "I-I don't think so. Are you?"

"I'm not sure—no, I don't think I am."

"Oh, we've got to do something!" Fay exclaimed, her voice shaking.

My heart was beating rapidly. "Y-Yes. I think we're going to have to go in."

Fay looked at me, her blue eyes wide open.

"B-But, that's extremely dangerous," Fay stammered.

I nodded. "I know, but we have to stop them! At least they seem to be done breaking windows."

"True, but we're not even teenagers yet! How can we, "a couple of giggling schoolgirls," stop criminals?"

I knew Fay had a point. My mind seemed to be going in circles. We couldn't let Uriah and that other person get away, but at the same time, if we went into the school building, we could be in serious danger.

What would Dad and Mom say? Would they want me to go in? Should I go get help?

The pressure was giving me a headache, but that was the least of my concerns.

I then noticed Fay peering through an unbroken window.

She was gripping tightly onto the window frame, an emotion on her face I couldn't quite place.

Unexpectedly she quickly ducked under the window. She then quietly inched away from the wall of the schoolhouse, and over to where I was.

I could see the fear on Fay's face as she said in a whisper, "Lia, we have to go in there!"

"W-What's happened?" I whispered back, my slightly stuttering voice sounding a little pathetic.

"Someone's in there!"

"Like a captive?" I asked, a sinking feeling in the pit of my stomach.

"Something like that, I think," replied Fay. "Oh, we've got to help!"

I nodded. "And there isn't time to lose! How are we going to get in, though? Obviously, we can't just walk in…"

Fay suddenly brightened like a light bulb and said, "Maybe not; but we can climb in!"

Before I knew it, Fay was hurrying over to the other side of the building. I watched, mouth hanging opened slightly, as Fay pushed herself up and over into the school, courtesy of the broken window. She didn't even mind the broken glass around the window seals threatening to cut her.

Fay peeked out of the window.

"Come on, Lia!" she whispered.

Trying my best to push away all fears, I too was soon climbing through the window.

I quickly tiptoed over to the slightly ajar door that led out of the classroom. As we stuck each of our heads out, Fay and I looked both ways to make sure Uriah and his comrade weren't in sight. The coast was clear.

Then I realized something.

"Fay," I began in a whisper, "where are we supposed to go?"

"I'll show you—it's across the hallway," replied Felicia just as quietly back.

As we quietly pushed open the door, each of us sneaking into the hallway, I held my breath, hoping we wouldn't get caught.

Fay signaled for me to follow her. Carefully, we made our way across the hallway. The once-familiar school now transformed into something strange and creepy. It was so empty. I wished I was just home, but there was no way I was backing down.

I'm going to be in big trouble when Grandmother finds out what Fay and I have been up to...

Trying to shake off the dread, I put my mind on the task at hand.

It was at that moment when Fay and I heard one of the doors down the hallway open.

Fay turned to me, her face full of horror.

"Turn back!" she hissed.

There was quite a bit of scurrying into the nearest room, and it was a wonder no one heard us.

We ended up hiding behind the door. I was silently hoping that whoever was out there would not come into this room. For one, we would most likely get caught, and for two, there was a big chance we'd get slammed in the face when the door got opened.

Fay and I heard footsteps walking toward the door. They were getting closer and closer... I was holding my breath and scrunching my eyes closed.

I was sure the doorknob was going to turn; I didn't dare look.

Then the footsteps stopped altogether. Whoever was out there seemed to be standing right outside the door.

It felt like hours of just waiting, wondering where those footsteps were going to go. I was gritting my teeth. Tension seemed thick in the air.

At last, I heard the footsteps had begun again. They seemed to be walking away. I slowly let out a big breath of relief. Fay did the same.

As Felicia and I exchanged glances, we both knew what the other was thinking. We needed to continue!

Carefully, we opened the door very quietly. Making sure the coast was clear, we began to make our way through the hallway again.

Only moments later, we were standing in front of a door.

Fay turned to me.

"This is it," she whispered. "This is the door."

I nodded.

"Ready?" I asked, feeling nervous.

"Yes," replied Felicia.

There wasn't a moment to lose. My hand shakily grabbed the doorknob… it was locked.

Oh no.

However, Fay didn't let that stop us. Before I knew it, she was hurrying down the hallway, leaving me by myself.

I was just standing there unsure what to do.

Only moments later, Fay came rushing down the hallway, trying her best to remain quiet.

When she was back by me, she showed me her clenched fist. Opening her hand, I saw a key.

"Hopefully this works," she whispered. "I found it in the principal's office. We'll return it, of course, but I doubt anyone would mind us using it under these circumstances."

I nodded, and Fay handed me the key.

Holding my breath, I tested the key. I sighed in relief once it successfully worked. Gripping the doorknob, I turned it, ready to go inside no matter what.

* * *

Pushing the door open, Fay and I looked around the room in the dim light.

"Oh, girls! I *am* so glad to see you."

Fay and I gasped at the voice.

"What happened?" asked Fay. "How did you get in here?"

"I'll tell you in a moment—hurry, hurry, before they come back and see you!"

Fay and I quickly slipped inside and closed the door.

Now that we were in the room, Fay said again, no louder than a whisper, "What has happened?"

There was a choke of a sob, which then became full-blown weeping, and a miserable and emotional voice said, "Oh, I have been betrayed!"

Fay and I exchanged troubled glances, and I stepped toward the weeping figure.

"Please don't sob," I begged. "They'll hear you."

The figure considered that and quieted down a great deal, much to my relief.

Fay came over and, still trying to figure out what was fully going on, said again, "Miss Caden, please, how did you get in here?"

I nodded. "Yeah, please tell us what happened."

"Here, darling," said our teacher. "Please untie this."

I looked at the rope tied around Miss Caden's wrists and began trying to pry the knots loose.

Miss Caden heaved a sigh. "Uriah had been acting strange, you know, and when you mentioned the abandoned building, Lydia, I knew I had to find out what was going on…"

I nodded, concentrating on the knots.

My teacher cleared her throat a little and then continued, saying, "I was about to leave the school this evening, after straightening up, but Uriah and some other man were there at the entrance and locked me in this room. So ruthless!"

"That's horrible!" exclaimed Fay.

"We have to do something!" I said firmly. "There, I untied you."

"Oh, thank you, darling," said Miss Caden, now freed from the rope. "Yes, girls, but what ever shall we do?"

We all were quiet for a moment, thinking.

At last, Miss Caden said, "Oh, girls, I got an idea."

"Really?" asked Fay. "What is it?"

"First, we need to get out of here," said my teacher. "I'll explain on the way. Oh, I do hope it works."

* * *

That's how I found myself, moments later, hurrying out of the school as fast as I could. Fay had quickly returned the key to the principal's office on the way out.

I was so worried we'd run into Uriah and his comrade. However, by some good fortune, the coast was clear.

I heaved a sigh of relief when Miss Caden, Fay, and I stepped out into the night. We hadn't been caught!

We snuck off the school property, and moments later, we were all hiding in the shadows.

"Miss Caden," began Fay, "what is your plan?"

"Well, we need to go back to that abandoned building you darlings told me about," said my teacher.

"Really?" I asked. "How come?"

Miss Caden smiled reassuringly in the moonlight. "While I was trapped, I overheard Uriah telling that other person they would go to his house around one thirty tonight. According to my watch, it is almost that late. I don't know how much time we'll have at the building; I imagine Uriah and his comrade are coming back. But I think they have something important in there."

Felicia slightly gasped. "Oh, then we need to hurry!"

I nodded. "Yes. We need to go right now!"

"My thoughts exactly," agreed Miss Caden. "Let's go."

We began to make our way around the town as fast as we could, ignoring the cold and snow.

I certainly hadn't expected to be rushing through Wilsonville past one in the morning with my teacher and Fay, but I was definitely glad not to be alone.

A little while later, the three of us were standing in front of the abandoned building. It felt like an eternity since Fay and I were here, but in reality, I imagined it wasn't more than two hours.

Miss Caden, Fay, and I quickly began to peek through the windows.

Looking through one of the cracked windows, Fay said, "No one's in there; the coast is clear."

Miss Caden heaved a sigh of relief. "Good. Then let's go, darlings."

We quietly but quickly got to the front door, and I grabbed the doorknob.

"Great," I began sarcastically, "it's locked..."

Miss Caden nodded. "Let's try the backdoor."

So, we headed to the back of the building. Upon reaching it, I tested the doorknob. Then, to my relief, it turned, and the door opened with ease—creaking rather loudly, however.

As it turns out, the door wasn't the only thing that squeaked. Old, wooden floors that led down the hallway creaked beneath our feet when we stepped inside.

I saw cobwebs on the walls and ceiling, as well as frayed curtains.

I noticed, just off the hallway, the huge window I had seen earlier that night. It was about seven feet tall or so, and about four feet wide. It was enormous compared to the other windows! It had a few cracks in it and was dirty, but it appeared higher in quality than the other windows.

"Where do we go, Miss Caden?" I asked.

"Let's try this room," replied my teacher, motioning to a room a little way down the hall, on the left.

The room itself was small. It had blinds on the window, which were closed. There was a wooden, reddish-brown desk. There was also a filing cabinet which was in one of the room's corners. Both pieces of furniture appeared to be old.

Miss Caden went to the filing cabinet and tried to open the top drawer, but it was locked. However, the ones below it weren't, so she searched those.

I then looked at the desk. It was tidy for the most part. There were a couple of drawers attached to it though, and I opened them.

Inside one drawer was a small pile of papers, and in the other were staples, tape, pencils—stuff like that.

I lifted up the papers in the one drawer, but I didn't see anything in it. I then decided to search the other drawer.

As I was doing so, Fay came over to the drawer of papers and pulled out the paper stack. She held the stack by one edge and then began shaking the papers. Her test proved useful as a silver key fell from the stack.

"Sharp as a tack, Fay," I said with a smirk. Since Cody is the one who usually says that phrase, I slightly frowned after.

Fay smiled a half smile, and she handed me the key.

Going toward the cabinet, I said, "Maybe this will work?"

Miss Caden smiled. "Oh, good!"

I stuck the key into the keyhole and hoped for the best. Turning the key, I beamed.

"It worked!" I cheered.

Opening the top drawer, I peeked inside. There were loads of papers!

"Miss Caden," I asked. "What are we looking for, exactly?"

"Yeah," Felicia said, also peeking into the drawer.

"We're looking for some very important papers," explained our teacher. "They'll most likely be in here."

Tilting her head a little to the side, Fay asked, "What kind of papers?"

"Well, you know what?" said Miss Caden. "Let's just grab all of these. Will you grab the briefcase over there, Lydia?"

I looked to where Miss Caden was pointing and saw a plain, black briefcase.

"Sure."

I retrieved the case and handed it to my teacher.

"Thank you, darling," Miss Caden replied, unzipping the case.

Nothing was inside the briefcase; Miss Caden started grabbing the big piles of papers, putting them inside. She had set the briefcase down on the floor. Fay and I also began putting the papers in the briefcase.

However, as we were grabbing the papers, one fell from Fay's stash and landed at my feet.

"Oh!" I exclaimed, picking it up. "I guess you dropped this."

Miss Caden was about to grab it gently from my hands, but I looked at the paper closely, narrowing my eyes.

"Darling?" asked Miss Caden. "What is it?"

Possibly an entire stack of proof, and I'm about to let it go to waste!

I quickly dropped down to my knees, about to start searching the other papers in the briefcase.

However, before I had the chance, Miss Caden roughly grabbed the paper I was holding and put it in with the others. She shut the briefcase.

I thought I had just seen a *big* clue written on one of those papers.

"Uriah could be back soon," she said briskly. "We have what we need. Let's go."

"Wait!" I shouted. "What's in there?"

"Why, proof, of course!" replied my teacher.

"Yeah," I said, a slight scoff in my voice. "But about *whom?*"

"Uriah," said Miss Caden quickly. "Let's go!"

"No!" I yelled. "I doubt that's *quite* the truth."

Fay tilted her head, baffled. "What is it you don't want us to see?"

"Why, nothing, unless it puts you in danger!" replied Miss Caden.

"Show us what's inside," Fay said.

Miss Caden sighed in exasperation and rolled her eyes. "When will you learn that you shouldn't play detective, *children?*"

My eyes widened, and Fay gasped.

Before I knew it, my friend took a step forward toward Miss Caden, totally aggravated. That was one of Fay's flaws; she had a feisty temper, which could get her into trouble.

"*Excuse* me?" Fay retorted. "As far as I can see, you're hiding something important! What is it?"

"Oh, girls," sneered Miss Caden, "it's about time you *finally* made the connection. I thought I taught you to be smarter than this."

"Tell me what you did!" I yelled.

Miss Caden smiled in a sick manner. "Let's just say I *never* forgave your mother when my grandfather passed away, Lydia."

Fay and I both gasped.

"T-That wasn't even Mom's fault!" I shouted, lamely stuttering some.

"It was as far as I'm concerned. She failed to help him get well," replied Miss Caden.

When Fay found her voice, she burst out, "No one could!"

I nodded in agreement. "He was sick! She helped him as much as she was able to!"

"It wasn't enough," said Miss Caden. "Now, if you'll excuse me, I have to go."

In an instant, Miss Caden was out of the room— and with the briefcase full of evidence!

Of course, Fay and I darted after her.

I managed to sprint fast enough to get to Miss Caden. I quickly gripped her wrist as hard as I could, and I yanked her to a stop. Fay grabbed Miss Caden's other wrist.

We were now in the room with the huge window.

"You did everything for a grudge!" I yelled to Miss Caden, fuming and upset. "You killed Mom and Dad just for revenge!"

"I brought justice!" Miss Caden retorted in anger.

Rage was bubbling up inside me, but I tried to ignore it for now. There had to be a way we could keep Miss Caden from escaping!

I was looking around the room wildly, trying to see if there was something I could use. I couldn't find *anything* in the bare room.

Before I knew it, though, glass was shattering everywhere! I closed my eyes tightly. Some glass hit me, and it hurt, but I had more pressing matters right now.

A moment later, I opened my eyes. Of course, I noticed glass was everywhere, and the huge window was broken. However, what I was really staring at was a jet-black horse in the room and its rider with strawberry-blond hair.

Then, I noticed several others outside dashing toward us.

"We're bound to win the next rodeo, Nightfall!" the strawberry-blond boy cheered. He was a little cut up from the shattered window but totally upbeat and bubbly.

"*Cody?*" Fay and I shouted in unison, very stunned and also very relieved.

Soon, I saw quite a few men sprint into the room. I recognized Mr. Blackwood, Mr. Nobleman, Ryker, Doctor Layton, Uriah, and also his comrade. There were also two other men I had never seen before.

Miss Caden then jerked free from my grasp and Fay's. However, she didn't get far, because before I knew it, Miss Caden was knocked to the ground by a flashlight.

Cody laughed in delight. "Nice throw, Fay!"

I suddenly realized that Fay threw the flashlight she got from her boot at Miss Caden. My eyes widened, but I nearly burst out laughing.

"Hop on, girls!" Cody shouted. "I'll explain everything at the house."

Realizing the others would get everything under control, I climbed up onto Nightfall.

* * *

Not too long later, I found myself sitting in the living room of Cody's house. Mrs. Nobleman was sitting on one of the leather couches, and we were waiting for Mr. Nobleman to come back with news. It was about three in the morning.

"So, how did you know to come to the abandoned building?" I asked Cody.

"Yeah, how?" inquired Felicia, yawning.

Cody smirked a little. "You'll never guess."

Curious, I replied, "What happened?"

Smirk growing, Cody said, "Trevin told me."

Fay and I both stared at Cody with wide eyes.

After a moment of shocked silence, Fay said, "Are you serious?"

"Yup!" Cody responded with a nod.

"But *how?*" I asked.

"Well, he threw rocks at the wall by my window until I woke up."

Fay laughed. "Then what happened?"

"When I woke up, I went downstairs and opened the front door. I asked him what he was doing at my house past one in the morning," explained Cody.

"He told me how he saw you guys up in the middle of the night and figured he'd tell me. When I asked him what *he* was doing out in the middle of the night, he told me to mind my own business."

I laughed. "That's Trevin all right."

Cody nodded with a snort. "Yeah, but I'm glad he told me about you guys."

Fay grinned. "That makes two of us."

"Three of us, actually," I said.

"Four," added Mrs. Nobleman.

Cody, Fay, and I laughed at that.

"So," continued Cody, "I was pretty sure you were going to the abandoned building. Obviously, I didn't want to miss out on the fun! Okay, okay, just kidding. I was a *little* worried."

Fay and I smiled.

Cody smiled back. "As it turned out, Ryker heard me up—must be a big brother thing—and I explained everything to him. Well, he went and woke up Dad and Mom. Dad and Ryker were going to go and check out the abandoned building. I wanted to go *really* bad, but Mom was worried it'd be dangerous, and Dad said I was too *young*."

"Then what happened?" I asked.

"Well," began Cody, "it turned out Uriah came to our house and told us about how Miss Caden actually murdered your parents, and I was so skeptical of him! But then he showed us proof. He actually was working undercover with everything shortly after he proposed to Miss Caden. I told Dad I could bring you two back to the house if they'd let me go with them on their search to find Miss Caden, since I figured you girls could be away from all the danger and stuff. Dad decided to let me go, which was awesome!"

Fay laughed a little. "Sounds like Lia and I weren't the only ones with a lot going on tonight."

Cody nodded. "No kidding. Anyway, Uriah, Dad, and Ryker jumped in my dad's pickup and started driving over to where you guys were. I got on Nightfall and took a shortcut and ended up getting to both of you at about the same time as the others. And, well, you know the rest."

Smirking, Fay said, "Only, you weren't able to stop very fast when you rode up to the building, so you ended up coming in through the window…"

"Yeah, my riding *may* have gotten a *little* out of hand," Cody said sheepishly. "I actually threw this rock that was in my saddlebag to break the window, seeing as I wasn't able to stop Nightfall in time. Thankfully, it didn't, like, hit you guys or anything."

Fay and I snickered at that.

Even though I uncovered the gloomy reason for my parents' death, I was glad the mystery had finally been revealed.

Lying sleepily on the couch, I frowned a little. My mother always worked hard as a nurse to restore the health of the sick. Years ago, when I was watching her work at Doctor Layton's clinic, Mother taught me you were never truly healthy unless you learned to forgive. Miss Caden proved to be an example of someone who appeared healthy, yet was ill.

It sure had been quite the night.

Springtime

Chapter 10

About a month later, the twentieth of March rolled around. It was the first day of Spring for 2004 and certainly a lovely day at that.

The last of the snow had melted away about two weeks earlier, and I was leaning against the abandoned bus, grinning. Fay was sitting on the bus steps, and somehow, Cody was sitting on *top* of the bus, his legs dangling over the edge.

Charity and Gopher were running around cheerfully, and Fay was holding Gracie in her arms.

"So," began Fay, "I wonder when we'll get our new teacher."

Cody shrugged. "Beats me."

Due to the fact Miss Caden was obviously not teaching us anymore, Fay's mother had temporarily taken up the role. She used to be a teacher before she got married and had a family, so she taught us well.

"We'll probably get one soon," I said.

Fay nodded. "Yeah. I wonder what the new teacher will be like."

Swinging his legs around happily, Cody said, "Maybe she'll be able to make me smart, like you are, Fay."

I laughed. "Well, from what I heard, your grades are already improving."

Cody nodded. "Yeah, Mrs. Blackwood is amazing!"

Felicia grinned. "I think so too."

I nodded in agreement. "Yeah!"

"Maybe your mom should just become our new teacher for good, Fay," Cody chirped.

Fay laughed. "She likes teaching us, but I think she wants to remain a housewife."

Kodiak nodded. "That's true."

We were quiet for a moment, but then we saw Ryker coming toward us.

Cody waved from his spot up on the bus's roof. "Hi, Pitchfork! What's up?"

Pitchfork—I mean, Ryker—laughed.

"Apparently, you are, Cross Eyes!" he shouted.

Fay and I couldn't stifle our giggles at all, and we burst out laughing and snorting.

Cody himself snorted and playfully rolled his eyes, saying, "Stereotypical giggling schoolgirls…"

We had shown the bus to Ryker about a month earlier, once we solved the mystery about my parents.

Ryker smirked. "The adults are about ready to head out. What about you guys?"

I nodded. "Sure!"

All of us were going on a picnic together. I was really excited about it. What a wonderful way to celebrate the first day of Spring!

Felicia stood up from the bus steps, brushing some dog hair off her yellow and gray shirt. She then set Gracie down.

"I'm ready to head out!" Fay said cheerfully.

Some of Gracie's dog hair blew over to where Cody was sitting on top of the bus, making him sneeze.

"I know you're shedding and all, but keep your dog dander to yourself, Gracie," Cody teased, climbing down the school bus.

Gracie just panted in response.

Ryker smirked. "Hey, Cody, I heard Mom made a batch of snickerdoodles for the picnic today. You guys are going to have to race me if you want there to be any left."

Instantly, Cody jumped off the bus and landed on the ground with a thud. He made a mad dash after Ryker, shrieking out, "You got a head start!"

Fay and I exchanged glances and with a laugh ran off after them.

* * *

"Ryker," Cody said, "are you going to ride with Fay and Lia and me?"

I was sitting in the Nobleman kitchen, munching on a snickerdoodle. All of us were about to leave for the picnic, and we were going somewhere else afterward. The place was a surprise.

Ryker shrugged. "Who are you riding with?"

Fay, who had been sipping some pink lemonade, said, "We're going with Lia's grandmother."

Smirking, Ryker teased, "Well, since I don't want Cody to be the only boy, and I want to ride in the convertible, I'll come too."

I laughed. "Grandmother's convertible is awesome!"

Felicia nodded and smirked slyly. "But now you'll have to be with *giggling schoolgirls.*"

Both Ryker and Cody playfully moaned.

"Oh, *no,*" Cody wailed dramatically. "They'll never stop snorting and screeching!"

"I agree," teased Ryker. "It'll be *so* excruciating!"

"We don't screech!" Fay and I retorted, playing along.

"Well," said Cody, "maybe it's more like laughing."

I rose an eyebrow at my strawberry-blond friend. "Seriously?"

"Yeah," said Cody, his older sibling nodding in agreement.

Ryker turned to Cody. Smirking, he said, "Well actually, now that I remember it, *you* certainly screeched last week, Cross Eyes, when you tripped on your spurs."

Cody gasped, betrayed. Pretending to be mad, he crossed his arms over his chest and turned on his heel abruptly.

"Come on, girls, let's go!" he shouted, storming out of the kitchen—and grabbing the basket of snickerdoodles as he left.

Fay and I laughed.

Grinning, I told Fay, "I guess we'd better go before Cody eats all the cookies."

* * *

Not that long later, we had spread out a couple of lovely, red, gingham picnic blankets and were about to enjoy a nice lunch of coleslaw, sandwiches, and watermelon, as well as a cheeseball—and of course, snickerdoodles.

As we were setting stuff up, I noticed that a couple of men were walking toward us. I instantly recognized them.

"Oh, look!" I exclaimed. "Here comes Uriah with his friend."

Grandmother laughed. "What do you think, Lydia? We invited them too but wanted to keep it a secret."

By the look on Kodiak and Felicia's faces, I could tell they hadn't known about this surprise either.

I still hadn't learned the name of Uriah's comrade, as I hadn't seen him since the night Fay and I learned that Miss Caden was guilty.

Just a moment later, we were all together, and there were greetings and shaking of hands. Before I knew it, I was meeting Uriah's friend.

The man had light-blond hair, pale-blue eyes, freckles, and a warm smile. I smiled back.

"Hello," I said. "I'm Lydia Arlington."

The man nodded and grinned a little.

"And I'm Adam Bennet."

My eyes widened at the name, and I was speechless for a moment.

"Wait—I'm sorry; I might have heard you wrong," I said.

"I think you may have heard me right," replied the man with a smile. "I said I'm Adam Bennet."

I stared at him in shock for a moment.

"Were you… my father's best friend?" I asked.

Adam nodded and softly smiled. "That's correct."

Slowly, a large grin spread across my face. "It's so nice to meet you!"

"It's nice to meet you as well, Lydia," said Adam. "Well, I actually met you a long time ago, but that was too long in the past for you to remember."

Fay smiled. "Oh, this is like a happy reunion!"

I nodded in agreement, beaming.

Cody was happily talking to Uriah, and I could tell that he already considered him a friend. As the two saw Adam, Fay, and me talking, they came over to us; this way, they could join in on the conversation.

I noticed that the others went over to the picnic spot so that they could finish setting up everything.

Uriah smiled at us. "I'm glad the mystery is finally solved."

"I am too," I said. I then looked a little sheepish. "However, Miss Caden almost escaped because I cut her ropes and all of that…"

Uriah nodded. "Yeah, but… you didn't know she was a criminal."

Felicia also looked a little sheepish. "We actually thought *you* were guilty."

Uriah laughed. "Well, I guess I did look pretty suspicious when I was watching you guys from my truck."

"I would have thought Uriah was untrustworthy," said Adam.

"I was actually just trying to make sure all of you guys were safe, but I guess I made you think I was up to no good."

Turning to Uriah, I said with a smile, "You had your own mystery to solve too."

Uriah nodded. "Yeah, shortly after I proposed, I felt something was off about my fiancée. As it turned out, I was right."

Cody laughed a little. "It sure is a good thing you realized who you were about to marry before you actually got hitched. That would have been really bad."

Adam nodded in agreement with Cody. "That's true. Thankfully, we found everything out."

Fay and I had already apologized to the others for sneaking out and causing all the ruckus. However, we still needed to apologize to Uriah and Adam.

Shuddering a little, Fay said, "Just think: We helped Miss Caden, and she nearly escaped with all the evidence against her!"

"Yeah," I said, remembering the briefcase Miss Caden almost ran off with. "I'm *really* sorry about almost ruining everything."

"So am I," apologized Fay.

"It's okay, girls," replied Adam.

Uriah smirked. "You were on the right track about someone being guilty; you just suspected the wrong person."

Fay and I laughed at that. "True."

Miss Caden had been taken away to stand trial. Of course, she was convicted without trouble. She had committed the crime against my parents at the aquarium. I can't imagine why she stayed in Wilsonville afterward, however. Why would she continue to live where she committed a crime?

We later found out that Miss Caden was the one who shattered the windows at the school. I still don't know how she did so, however.

I was still feeling glum, but I was trying to push forward. Dad would always say we shouldn't get completely wrapped up in the past; we needed to work toward a happy future, he believed. I still really miss my parents, though.

"So," said Adam, "try to be a little more careful next time."

Fay and I nodded seriously.

"We were rash..." I said.

Cody suddenly grinned. "Yeah, but I do still laugh when I remember how Fay threw that flashlight at Miss Caden."

I snickered, and Fay smirked.

"It had to be done," said Fay with a laugh.

Adam then grinned and whispered to me, "Besides, Caden's face was priceless."

* * *

"It's such a lovely day for a picnic, isn't it?" asked Mrs. Nobleman.

Grandmother and Mrs. Blackwood nodded. "Yes, it is."

I thought it was a wonderful day as well. Swirly clouds were in the blue sky. Cheerful dandelions were growing. There was a slight breeze, and the weather was sunny. I felt sunny inside too. The troubles that had been weighing down on me so much before now seemed far away.

Fay beamed. "I can't wait to swing."

Cody and I looked with longing eyes at the swings a little way off. All of us love to swing. Even Ryker joins us sometimes.

I grinned happily. "I also can't wait; it's been too long."

Cody nodded wholeheartedly, chomping on a watermelon slice. "Agreed!"

Ryker looked at the three of us and smirked. "Why don't we just go right now?"

Instantly, we were asking the adults if it was okay, and with their approval we were hopping on the swings.

It was very fun, and we tried to see who could swing the highest. Fay ended up winning against us, which surprised Ryker, Cody, and me. But when Cody insisted we should try *standing* on the swings, we all knew to change the subject.

I loved feeling the breeze as I swung, and I loved the sunny weather too. I smiled softly as I remembered how my father used to push me on these swings years ago.

In the distance, I could see the adults talking amongst themselves. Soon, they were walking over toward us, and we jolted our swinging to a halt. We stood up, a little curious.

Grandmother smiled at us. "We're about ready to head out for that mini trip we planned. What about you four? Are you ready?"

Ryker, Cody, Fay, and I all nodded in unison, saying, "Yeah!"

That had the others laughing a little.

As we headed out of the park, I smiled, ready to find out just where I was about to go.

* * *

I hadn't known where I was going, but that only added to the fun of the ride. Ryker was sitting in the passenger's seat up front, leaving the backrow for Cody, Fay, and me. There had been a lot of debate on who should sit where, and I eventually ended up sitting in the middle. The middle seat has always been my favorite when Cody and Fay drive with us because I'm happily sandwiched between my two best friends.

It had been a pretty long drive, but as we drove, I eventually realized we were in Ashland.

Before I knew it, I could see a very familiar place come into sight.

When the convertible pulled up to this very familiar place, I gasped, and Cody and Fay were grinning.

Grandmother parked and shut off the car. She turned toward us. "Surprise!"

I saw the others already parked and grinning— well, except for baby Leanne, since she didn't really know what was going on.

Before I knew it, I was scrambling out of the convertible and giving Grandmother a huge hug.

ABOUT THE AUTHOR

DANIELLE RENEE WALLACE is a teenage author born in Washington State. She established a large love for reading during her elementary school years and a strong love for writing while in middle school. At fourteen, Danielle published her first book, while living in Lubbock, Texas. Her father spent about one year of his boyhood in Wilsonville, Nebraska, the town in which Danielle's series, *Secrets of the Abandoned Bus,* takes place. Currently, she resides in northern Ohio with her parents and two older brothers.